groundwater

a collection of contemporary
Kentucky fiction

edited by
Scot Brannon
Marguerite Floyd
Charlie Hughes

The Lexington Press, Inc.
Lexington, Kentucky
1992

Copyright © 1992 by The Lexington Press, Inc.

First edition.

All rights reserved.

Complete acknowledgements appear at end of book.

All inquiries and permission requests should be
addressed to The Lexington Press, Inc.,
P.O. Box 11365, Lexington, KY 40575

ISBN 0-9628089-1-1

Printed in the United States of America.

Contents

3   Kentucky Eclectic: Stories for Now
      Leon V. Driskell

9   The Assumption of Father O'Roon
      Constance Alexander

23   Hellcat
       Garry Barker

32   Descent from Avernus
       Chris Beyers

45   Beach Drums
       Marjorie M. Bixler

54   The Terrorist
       Pat Carr

59   Lawrence & Aletha
       Chris Holbrook

68   The Kentucky River
       Martin Kent

80   Quiet Down, Quiet Down
       Michele Moore

91   Making It Through the Night
       Barbara Presnell

98	from "Scenic Roots" Deborah Reed
107	Blood for Blood Henry Riekert
115	The Ghost of the Piano Peggy Steele
122	Barking Dogs David Stewart
133	One Main Sound Mary Ann Taylor-Hall
144	Reflections on an Abandoned House Jesse James Once Supposedly Slept In Allison Thorpe
149	About the Authors
152	Acknowledgements

groundwater

Kentucky Eclectic: Stories for Now

No formula shaped this collection of stories. No editor stamped it with a single-minded theory of what fiction is, or should be. From all over Kentucky, these stories came together at the office of the lately fledged Lexington Press in response to a printed call for submissions. From over two-hundred submissions, The Lexington Press has selected fifteen stories by nine women and six men. This eclectic collection is as diverse as the people who constitute Kentucky today.

The solicitation flyer addressed "Kentucky Fiction Writers," and it asked them quite simply, "Just send us your best." No restrictions on theme or content, flexible length requirements (five to twenty pages). The flyer stipulated that writers must live in Kentucky, but it made no requirements that the stories reflect "the Kentucky experience."

Groundwater follows an earlier Lexington Press book, *Through the Gap*, a sampling of work by thirty-six Kentucky poets. Both books are printed on recycled, acid-free paper in paperback (thus affordable) format. Publication of *Groundwater* leaves no doubt that the founders of The Lexington Press are dead serious about their purposes: "the encouragement of diversity in literature from all areas of Kentucky" and "the general promotion of quality literature."

I am proud to have the opportunity to introduce this book to readers. In the pages that follow appear stories that differ widely in mode and tone, setting and technique. They have in common seriousness of purpose, nowhere more apparent than in the comic stories, and denial of the easy and facile effect. Something important happens in all these stories, but that "something" never arises from mere plot contrivance. These fictions remind me that a story requires a story-teller and a listener; hence, I become an agent in the achievement of the stories. Just by listening.

Listen to these stories.

Peggy Steele's "The Ghost of a Piano" amounts to a prose meditation, but one hears the poet in the selection and ordering of the experiences told. The familiar, so common some people don't see it, evokes the poet: "The kudzu disappears each December without a trace, but like all things so delicate that bulldozers don't apply, it finds a way each spring to lift its flat leaves, not very high off the ground. Rippling like water in the sunlight, it keeps green the piano's ghost, lying under that ground like springwater waiting to be tapped."

Henry Riekert's "Blood for Blood" achieves something of the austerity of the best of tragedy. It is as absolute as scripture, and brings to mind a morality play, an Everyman's story of our dark and bloody century.

Michele Moore's "Quiet Down, Quiet Down" works wonderfully on the comic level, but achieves new depths when the sleep-deprived Doris drifts into dream. She is a medical transcriber contending with the necessity to get all records into shape for an inspection, but the nocturnal moanings of a dog named Duke prevent her sleeping. Her dreams combine the frustration of her work, and the madness of black sheep raining down from the sky, a child screaming, and a "familiar wailing, like a donkey gone mad" — Duke, of course, whose moans wake her again. Moore's story, like the work of a good stand-up comedian, depends upon its timing, its subtle undercutting of what gets too close to the nerve.

Some of the stories in *Groundwater* name specific locals but do not depend on region as such. In "Making It Through the Night," Barbara Presnell does not localize Rosajohn's home, but mentions that Rosajohn and Sam had once lived in Virginia. Rosajohn is spending her first night alone, while her son Joey spends the night with his father. The marriage has broken up: "Sometimes Rosajohn thinks the real reason she and Sam split was food . . . Irreconcilable differences in the blood stream, she pictures herself saying to the judge." Presnell keeps her focus sharply on Rosajohn, never interpreting or judging. The story provides, without a clinical smell, a painful study in the pathology of love.

Others of the stories in *Groundwater* grow from recognizable Kentucky soil, and take full advantage of the regional. Garry Barker's "Hellcat" allows plenty of smiles and several laughs before his fantastically elaborated story takes its final and serious turn.

Martin Kent's "The Kentucky River" occurs more recently than "Hellcat," but its central character also suffers what society judges to be disabling deficiencies. Kent's story opens with a promise of humor: "Mike was standing in his Aunt Mabel's overgrown backyard with his pants and underwear down around his ankles. Two hours before that, he had swallowed a small, black pill that Billy Carpenter had sold him for two dollars, telling him it was black mescaline." Mike's naked march to town and into the bank affords additional moments of potential humor, but laughs are not what this story is about. Kent allows the reader to hear the words of an autobiographical essay Mike wrote as part of his treatment during a brief stay at a Drug and Alcohol Abuse Center in Louisville. The boy's childlike good will, his love of a good time ring true, but his estimate of the world he lives in is at sad variance with the facts.

Chris Holbrook characterizes an aging farm couple with a wealth of details about the work they do. In "Lawrence and Althea," Holbrook shifts his focus from wife to husband and back again with a bare minimum of dialogue. The story opens with a pack of wild dogs trying to get at Althea's chickens. Lawrence, obviously the weaker of the two, is resting, and tells his wife, "They ain't a bit of danger . . . Them dogs are bluffed of you." Not only do the dogs turn out to be ferocious, but there are other predators as well: something has been at Althea's tomatoes (a muskrat, says Althea; a turtle, says Lawrence), and worms' nests cover the limbs of the winesap trees. At first, Lawrence merely goes through the motions of defending their livelihood, but after nearly everything goes wrong, he realizes it's up to him to set things right. He is doing just that when, at the story's end, the rain he had said earlier would "be good for everything," finally sets in.

Allison Thorpe's "Reflections on an Abandoned House Jesse James Once Supposedly Slept In" comes to glorious life when the contemporary narrator's mind "is flung to a time before the oozing asphalt, the machine violations, the three-bedroom bricks . . ." The story joins Jesse James fleeing from pursuers and into an exuberance of green and of lilacs in an otherwise "brown and thirsty" landscape where "locusts rule the world" and "creeks lie dead as the animals that go there to die." The blind old woman who lives in a house swallowed in lilacs takes the bandit in. She longs for death, to join her husband and dead children, and what transpires between her and Jesse James strikes truer than textbook history.

Deborah Reed draws the reader into an excerpt from her "Scenic Roots" this way: "The bombs had missed her. She was still alive. She dragged herself along the edge of the jungle using her elbows for leverage, planning her tombstone as she went. 'Youngest Air Force Hero Ever,' it would say. 'A courageous spy shot down in the line of duty saving countless women and children.' " The date: July 1971.

Reed's protagonist, like most of us back then, is confused about Vietnam. She lives in a confusing world of crazy grown-ups and taunting children. Molly, the girl becoming a woman, never becomes a "narrative device." She is a personality. Molly sitting ingloriously in the mud of a hog wallow. Molly painting a picture of a beautiful woman in an emerald dress. Molly trying to understand the hatred, the anger around her. The narrator tells us: "Time has a way of bumping forward for Molly almost as giddy and quick as it slides into memory."

Constance Alexander's "The Assumption of Father O'Roon" allows the reader to infer an entire community of which Father O'Roon and a young woman named Elena are representatives. The action occurs in the church, where Father O'Roon (though he longs for his sherry) has waited in order to hear Elenda's confession. The story title's irony, its play on the usual religious meaning of assumption, opens the way for recognition of further ironies. Father O'Roon's final gesture — placing coins in the poor box — seen in the light of what he has learned will seem grotesquely inadequate to most readers. Alexander resists judgement, even innuendo.

Marjorie Bixler's "Beach Drums" opens up a world of promise to her first-person narrator, but it forbids her enjoying, or even pursuing those promises. The narrator is caring for her niece Lisa at a beach resort in South Carolina, while her husband remains at work in the city. Her son is away at camp. A neighbor engages her and Lisa in conversation. Lisa, far from being a stage prop, establishes herself as wise in the ways of the world she and her aunt must occupy. The gentle and kind neighbor confesses he is jealous of his ex-wife's new husband because of his children, not his former spouse. The narrator fears to lose her son if she breaks free. Lisa's parents show up, raising the question of propriety about Joe's constant presence, and the narrator knows their "whole kingdom" is lost when a sand castle washes away.

One of the shortest of the fifteen stories is also among the most disturbing. Pat Carr's "The Terrorist" looks at the meaning and implications of the word compromise. The narrator sees a former student, Mohammed Sherif, on television news. He is being held for questioning in connection with a car-bomb explosion. She recalls Sherif's behavior in her class for foreign students. Without straying from her narrative, Carr forces the reader to question whether the fanatic is, in fact, simply a person of principle. Questions of right and wrong multiply, and none of the questions has an easy answer.

In "Descent from Avernus," Chris Beyers manages to turn an amusing, even ludicrous story of a widowed man who seeks to avoid reunion with his wife after death into a withering portrait of a marriage. He sets out comically to avoid heaven, but his sins have a way of slipping away from him, or turning into virtues. A passage in St. Mark convinces him that his unremitting hatred of his dead wife assures his damnation. That comfort turns into a double-edged sword when he sets to thinking about his marriage. Compulsively, he works out the rest of his fate through symbolic logic. Not Mrs. Medwin, but he, stands in need of forgiveness: he is the source of his misery and hers as well. Avernus is the Roman entrance to the underworld. Perhaps Mr. Medwin descends from Avernus because he has found hell within himself.

David Stewart's "Barking Dogs" comes close to defying description. It depends less upon its apparent Asian jungle setting than upon the extension of a metaphor implicit in the story's first sentence: "The mountain was the only place he felt comfortable." He, variously known as Preacher Man, Zeus, and Son of Cronos, wants the long view of things. On the mountain, "his throne was a solid, living rock," and what's more ". . . he could see forever." The reader scarcely knows how to take the Olympian imagery. As the horrific action progresses, Preacher Man hears, or imagines he hears, dogs barking. He recalls a French balloonist's statement "in the early days of manned flight that a dog's bark was the last sound heard at great heights." Other Olympian figures intrude in the story, and, and after learning something of Preacher Man's background, the reader jolts from the lofty heights to another setting and another view of Preacher Man.

No story in my recent experience has reached the magnitude and the sheer emotional force of Mary Ann Taylor-Hall's "One Main Sound." I could say that "One Main Sound," like Peggy Steele's "The Ghost of the Piano," is about music, and that would be true. I could say it is about loss and grief, and that, too, would be true. "One Main Sound" is also about love, and how love sometimes demands physical expression before it can be recognized.

Perhaps my best statement about Taylor-Hall's story is that it is about the creation and our participation in it: "There's one main light in the world; everything we call color is a splitting apart of this one light. So I thought maybe there might be one great chord, too, like the light of the sun, that separates into the notes of the world. Creation would be the splitting apart of this chord. Music would come out of it, every note, every harmony. Music would also try to get back to it." A brisk narrative tells Karin's experience, her efforts to merge with that great chord and to locate her lost child somewhere beyond the rocks. The story frightens, even as it thrills. Hearing this story is to share its religious experience, back in the real world of the sense where time opens out even as it limits:

> I opened my eyes then and saw all there was to see. Mackerel clouds, converging to a point in the east. White cows with the last long light of the clear day making them glow against the fields as though lit from underneath. The beginning pink of the sunset, over on the other side.

Listen to all these stories. They will stay with you.

Leon V. Driskell
Louisville, Kentucky

The Assumption of Father O'Roon
Constance Alexander

It seemed she was not going to show up after all. He might have guessed. She was probably embarrassed to face him, but a note from her might be tucked beneath the amber glass of sherry that awaited him in the rectory. Such missives were often Elena's way of escaping his counsel.

Father O'Roon peered at his watch in the murky light of the confessional. He could barely see the two hands stretching between 6 and 12, like the thin silver rope that binds heaven to hell. Well, he had waited long enough.

He braced himself to rise from the wobbly bench, one elbow jutting through the cleft between the worn velvet curtains, the other nudging the brass crucifix on the opposite wall. When he heard the gentle push of knees on the padded *prie dieu* in the adjoining booth, he smirked and then wiped it quickly. She had not stood him up after all.

As if Elena could see him through the closed partition, O'Roon paused for a long-suffering glance heavenward. He reopened his prayer book with pious deliberation, balanced it on his stiff knee, and readied himself to greet the fugitive from God's grace who knelt on the other side.

He waited before sliding the screen open. Let her think he had not heard her. Let *her* wait.

She risked a tiny cough.

O'Roon held his silence.

The next cough was more deliberate. But he still lingered before parting the barrier between them.

Under any circumstances, he would have known it was Elena. The unmistakable scent of freshly ironed linen mingled with traces of brass polish. As usual, she was kneeling straight-backed, chin up, directly facing him. If there had been light, they might have looked at each other eye to eye.

"So?" O'Roon inquired in the same forbidding tone Mrs. Shaughnnessy used when answering the phone in the rectory. "Yes?"

He imagined that Elena's folded hands were moist with the secret she clutched. He knew when she spoke it might be with a stammer of guilt. That was often her way in the confessional. In such cases, he sometimes began with a kind question. But this time he let the silence settle. Let her plunge into the cold cleansing waters by herself.

"Bless me, Father." Elena rushed her whispered words with a Sign of the Cross. "It has been one week since my last confession. I accuse myself of . . . ."

Of course. She would resort to following the prescribed form. In the face of shame she would revert to chanting what she was taught as a child. Other weeks, her confession was more like a conversation, the two of them taking turns at asking and answering questions about the week's dose of imperfection.

O'Roon had administered the sacrament of reconciliation to the girl nearly every Saturday since he first came to the parish. He was the one who had manufactured a job for her back then. She had ironed the linen of the priests since she was ten; and in the past year, to justify a desperately needed raise in salary, O'Roon had elevated her duties to include preparing the altar for Sunday Mass while Saturday afternoon confessions were in progress. The young girl had been breathless with gratitude that still another task had been added to her already-long list of responsibilities. Besides that, she welcomed the opportunity to confess to O'Roon.

"What was that, my child?" As if he had not heard her. O'Roon's advancing age was a good excuse for making her repeat.

"I said I have committed a sin of pride, Father."

"Ah, pride." O'Roon repeated, nodding wisely as if she could see him through the drape of twilight. Pride indeed, he wanted to say. But O'Roon decided to let her run the drama according to her own script. "And how did this sin show itself?"

"I was the only one who could cite the scriptures Sister questioned us on in Bible History yesterday."

If she had told him this elsewhere, O'Roon might have clapped her on the back. He had coached her, after all; from the sound of things it had paid off. But today she chose to waste his time with a diversion. Let her play her little game, let her think she was fooling him.

"There is no sin in being a scholar," O'Roon reminded her in the voice he had used when he was principal of the boy's preparatory school. "Using intellectual gifts is just another way of worshipping Our Lord." O'Roon wondered if the girl realized that her position at the top of her class was mostly due to his tutelage.

"I know there's no sin in knowledge, Father. But I felt myself smiling with satisfaction when Sister singled me out for praise. I feel I must learn not to be so quick to take credit for the work of the Holy Spirit."

"I see. So are you going to take steps to curb the growth of intellectual arrogance?" O'Roon startled himself with the forgotten phrase. *Intellectual arrogance.* He had once been accused of such a crime in the seminary, but had never confessed it as a sin. Stupidity, after all, was a much worse offense.

"I started mending my ways as soon as I realized I was lacking humility, Father. I did not answer any questions in that class for the rest of the session. And I will resist raising my hand so much. I should give the others a chance, don't you think?"

"Perhaps," O'Roon hedged, wondering where she would go next with this evasion. "You might help the rest of your classmates more by *answering* Sister's questions," he chided. "You speak of the sin of pride. But is it not also a sin to reject the God-given gift of intelligence?" he asked as if he were genuinely puzzled.

"I did not think of that, Father. In a way, if I stop participating in class I am being selfish, I suppose."

"So you are saying that by not sharing your knowledge, you are sinning against others?"

"I did not say that, but I guess it is a valid point, Father." She still sounded unconvinced.

"Surely you realize the students listen to each other much more carefully than they do Sister. They can learn from you."

"I must think about that, Father. Thank you. I will ask the Blessed Mother for help with this. Too much humility may be self-serving, too. The difference between genuine humility and a false sense of piety is a subtle one, I suppose."

"Most subtle," O'Roon agreed wryly, but the girl seemed not to hear. She had already moved on to the next wrongdoing.

"Envy, Father. That is the next sin I need to confess."

"Ah, yes. Covetousness is a difficult sin to avoid in a world where the haves and the have-nots mingle so freely."

"That is so true, Father. I see the other girls. I want their pretty clothes. The jewelry. The pastel slippers some of them wear to Mass on Sunday."

"But God sees only how we have furnished our souls. These other things. They are frivolous. Don't you see?"

"Oh, yes, Father. I know that. When I stop and think, I realize how unimportant such finery is." She paused, and O'Roon thought he detected a slight frown on her face, but it was really too dark to be sure. "I saved up some money for ribbons for my hair," Elena went on. "Maybe I could do a good penance with it."

He found himself swallowing to quell his impatience. "And how is that, my child?" he managed innocently.

"I will put my coins in the box for special intentions, and I will light a candle so the Blessed Virgin will help me with this envy."

Again O'Roon squelched a retort. It was so like Elena to get him sidetracked, to hope that somehow they would get engaged in a conversation that would allow her to "forget" the real reason she was here. He silently congratulated the girl on her tactic. They had discussed the lighting of candles before. To O'Roon the action was irrelevant, almost irreverent, like placing a divine bet at the feet of the faded statue. But to the girl, the lighting of a candle held some divine mystery.

"So," he couldn't keep the tone of sarcasm out of his voice, "perhaps Mary will listen to your prayer more conscientiously if you couple it with a coin? Perhaps we can get our worst offenses pardoned if we pay the price of indulgence?" he prodded.

"That is not exactly what I meant, Father," Elena replied primly, and O'Roon could sense her urge to disagree with him on this question once again. "Such an offering is just a gesture after all, Father. A symbol for something larger."

He had to hand it to the girl. Perhaps some day they would end up laughing about her skill at distraction. Instead of prodding her onward, O'Roon decided to hold back still, even though thoughts of the waiting glass of sherry were beginning to draw a longing from him.

"You are saying, then," O'Roon went on, "that a primitive act of dropping a coin in the box and then lighting a candle has the same importance as, say, the symbolism of the parables?"

"I'm not sure. I must reflect on it, Father."

O'Roon had to smile to himself. She was exhibiting extraordinary stubbornness in her evasion. "So you will buy the ribbons?"

"Oh, no, Father. I said I would think of the relationship between lighting a candle and the parables. I *still* intend to offer my coins as part of my penance."

"So you will purchase no frippery with your treasure, but drop it in the poor box instead?"

"That is right, Father."

In the beat of silence that followed, O'Roon peered at his watch. It could be after midnight for all he knew. This child would try the patience of a saint. "Shall we go on?" he suggested brusquely.

"Yes, Father. To go on," Elena faltered, "it is something that I feel. You know how shy I am — I mean, I am shy, Father."

Clever, he thought. A good lead-in. "You say you are shy?" O'Roon prodded kindly, as if the girl's sudden stammer or her confused blushes in the face of strangers might vindicate her. "This is no sin as far as I know. Shyness, I mean. I think our Lord, Jesus, was probably a retiring person."

He expected she might be urged to disagree with this comparison between herself and Jesus, but instead there was only silence on the other side.

"Yes. I — I mean no, Father. What I want to say is that I feel myself wanting not to be so shy. Now that, in itself, is not a bad thing, but it could lead me into sin nevertheless. You see, Father?"

O'Roon nodded slightly, and cleared his throat. So she was finally going to get into it. He felt relieved. It was getting late, and he could almost taste the thick sweetness of the sherry. "Um hunh," he replied.

"Being shy has kept me from socializing," Elena went on. "That and my father. He is so strict that I never even think of talking to boys, except in school, of course."

"Yes?" O'Roon let the word hover. "So this is about boys."

"No. Well, not exactly. Actually, yes it is. There is a boy who pays attention to me. I know when he is looking at me. I can feel myself talking a little louder to my girlfriends when he is around. I want him to hear what I say, and think how smart and clever I am."

"Is there nothing more to this flirtation?" O'Roon congratulated himself on the genuine puzzlement he managed to convey. Of course he knew there was more, but let her be the one to own up. Let her say the sooty words herself.

O'Roon had seen the whole thing. A blind man could not have missed it. Was it possible she didn't realize?

He had been in the sacristy placing satin markers in the Missal when Tomas Sansome delivered the communion bread. Elena had finished polishing the chalice, and was laying out the vestments for Sunday Mass.

She tossed back her marvelous, thick hair when Sansome shuffled into the room and mumbled a hello, and then turned quickly to smooth the folds of an altar cloth. But not before O'Roon caught the burnished flush of pleasure on her face.

The image of Sansome seemed to crowd O'Roon's side of the confessional, making him shift on the hard wooden bench to find enough room for himself.

"I wouldn't call this a flirtation, Father. I'm just saying that I feel confused. I want this boy to notice me, but when he does I find I cannot speak. I just am — I don't know . . . ."

"Indeed." The word was intended to detour her wanderings. "Have you found yourself getting attention in other ways? Nonverbal ones?" O'Roon hunched forward, almost touching the screen with his forehead. Now he had her.

"I — I look at him when he's not aware. It works sometimes. He'll look up and catch me staring."

"And then what happens?"

"I look away. I'm embarrassed, you see."

"I see. Yes." He picked up the pace. "So we are here to talk of sinning. What wrongdoing is bothering you with this boy? If you don't talk to him, and only stare, where's the harm?" O'Roon paused, wondering if she would actually dare to lie in the confessional. "Is there some action that you have engaged in with this male? Something besides the staring, I mean?"

"Not an action, really, Father. Well, I guess it's kind of an action. Or non-action. Maybe it is a sin of omission." Her tone brightened for a second, and she sounded relieved that this misdeed might have such a name.

"There are such sins," O'Roon conceded. "They consist of

not doing something that you know you *should* do. Is there something like that bothering you?"

"Yes, Father. I knew you would be able to help me with this. It is something that happened today. With the boy I mentioned. The one I keep getting shy with?"

"Go on." O'Roon pulled his cuff back abruptly, to check the time once again. It was too dark to make any sense out of his watch. Father Perina might have already locked the gracefully curved bottle of sherry back in the liquor cabinet.

"Well today, Father, I saw that boy. And I had to lean towards him so he could hand me something."

"Yes?" O'Roon could see Elena's shoulders easing toward the boy, her outstretched arms ready to take the loaves of communion bread from Tomas Sansome.

"I accidentally brushed against him, Father."

O'Roon's silence nudged her forward.

"You see, Father, I touched him. And I did not move away."

O'Roon held his tongue as if it were a fragile wafer in his mouth. "So you bumped into this fellow?" he finally asked.

"Yes, Father.

"I am sorry. I am confused," the priest apologized. Just as he feigned not hearing, O'Roon occasionally risked a slight show of senility to chide the guilty. "Perhaps I let my attention slip for a moment. What is the sin in this kind of jostling?"

"The sin, Father — the omission, I believe you would call it — is that I liked touching him, so I did not rush to move away."

"I see, my child. But I still am not sure of the sin. The touching you are talking of . . . ."

"Yes, Father?"

"You have not told me the nature of this contact. This was not a kiss, or a caress. Am I right?"

"Yes, Father."

"So exactly what was it?"

"I brushed against him with my chest."

O'Roon could almost feel her wince as she waited for his reaction. "Your — chest?" The scene was etched in his mind, but of course he would not confess to the girl. Elena had leaned over Sansome for just an instant, her breasts nudging the boy's inner arm. Neither one of them moved for a second. If O'Roon had not been there in the background, getting the money from his worn purse to pay the boy, the two of them might still be riveted in that pose, locked forever in the delicious accident of contact.

"I liked that sensation, Father, and it shames me. I feel such actions could lead to other sins. I know it was not right. So that is why I am confessing it."

Perhaps it was compassion, or just the vision of the waiting glass of sherry, but O'Roon felt himself relenting. "It is wise to beg forgiveness for such incidents. You are right in recognizing that this could lead to more wrongdoing. You are a young girl, not yet ready for such encounters with a male. Your body is a sacred gift, not to be tampered with. You must remember that."

"I will, Father. I will not look at this boy any more. Whenever I think of him I will pray to the Blessed Virgin to give me the grace of her purity and modesty."

"Praying to the Virgin will help. Keeping busy with your studies is also another endeavor to occupy you. It sounds as if you are trying very hard to do the right thing, so let us finish up and—" O'Roon's hand was already raised to start the blessing.

"There is one other thing, Father."

O'Roon dropped his hand back to his lap and slumped tiredly before he spoke. The girl was really pushing him. "Yes?"

"I was not going to say anything, Father. But you have helped me so much today, to figure out what is right."

A sudden cramp in O'Roon's upper leg seized his attention. He desperately kneaded his thigh with his hand, nearly groaning, wanting to pound on it with his fist. He finally settled on straightening the leg, poking his foot beneath the curtain, and stretching it out into the aisle. He imagined the polished toe of his black shoe could trip any demons that lurked in the black stillness of the church.

"I must confess a sin that shames me in front of God Himself. I was not going to tell anyone. Even you, Father." The slight change in Elena's tone was a subtle shift to a lower pitched whisper. Her words melted into the darkness almost before O'Roon was able to decipher them.

"So?"

She must have sensed his growing impatience. "I have provoked the sin of lust." The syllables rustled like a silk petticoat.

"And how did you do this?"

"I am not sure, Father. My body has led to this sin, I am afraid."

O'Roon had, of course, noticed how Elena wore the mantle of womanhood, clutching it shyly to her body, but occasionally letting it slip off one shoulder.

"I have caused impure thoughts." She paused to take a deep breath. "And deeds."

"You cannot be responsible for another's thoughts. But deeds are another story, my child. With deeds there is complicity." Really, this false piety was something he was going to have to rid her of. "What are these 'deeds' you so obliquely mention?"

"I did not know what else to do, Father. If I had not caused the thoughts themselves, then there would have been no deeds to follow."

"I must understand these deeds, then. For I cannot grant absolution without knowing what sin it is I am forgiving."

"I allowed a male to touch me, Father." Her admission was muffled by the escape of a small sob.

"This is different from the act of omission you just described?"

"Yes, Father. It is different."

"So you allowed a man to touch you?"

"Yes." It was barely a whisper.

"On your private parts?"

"Yes, Father. My chest. And — and my, uh, be — between my legs."

The silence that floated between them swelled and pinked.

"So you allowed this violation?"

"Yes, Father."

"And you have come here to confess this sin and to receive absolution?"

Her answer was nearly lost in the clasped hands that she held in front of her mouth. "Yes."

"So a man has been permitted to touch your breasts? Willingly, on your part. No accident."

"Yes, Father."

"And he has fondled you — your genitals. In the place that only a husband should know."

"That is right."

"Have you agreed to other violations?"

She sniffed and coughed lightly before she answered.

"You mean, Father?"

"I mean, has there been intercourse?" O'Roon's voice, though still a whisper, was harsh.

"Yes, Father."

"And this was a willful act?"

"Not really, Father. What I mean is — it was not *my* will. But I felt that refusal was an even greater sin."

"What offense could be greater than violation? It is a mortal sin. A serious desecration of a young woman's purity. But you did it any way?"

"Yes, Father. But I truly did not want to."

"But you did want him to touch you. Your breasts. And the other?"

"I did not think of wanting that, Father. It never occurred to me. I know that my body is maturing. The men sometimes make jokes toward me. Sometimes the blouses I wear. The buttons...."

"So you are aware that you dress provocatively." It was not a question, but a statement of triumphant truth.

"It is not intentional, Father. We are poor. But..."

"'But' is just an excuse. You are a daughter of the Virgin Mary. You must practice modesty. It is not modest to make a display of yourself. In *any* way. To allow yourself to be used. Wearing tight clothing, this flirting. The — the sin of omission. And then this episode." O'Roon's voice ascended one step above a whisper. "It is not modest to allow your breasts to be fondled. It is how such sexual encounters begin."

She had been answering a "Yes, Father," to each of his statements, but he was no longer waiting for her response.

"So what am I supposed to think?" He had moved so close he could feel her shortened breath thorough the thin partition. Instead of speaking more quietly, his volume rose. "It seems you have deliberately provoked this action. Forcing a man into sinful deeds."

"I did not want to, Father. It — it had never happened this way before."

"Before!" O'Roon's volume climbed another notch. "What do you mean 'before?' This has been going on in the past? Or something leading up to this?" The prayer book that had been balanced on his right knee fell to the floor. "So you have been sneaking around and it is just now you are confessing your sins? And you have become so wantonly bold you would flaunt such an act in front of me in the sacristy? In the vestibule of the altar itself, where the Blessed Sacrament sits?" His voice shook with anger. The girl had deliberately performed in front of him. Probably trying to test his own vow of chastity.

The swift image of Tomas Sansome's slow, insolent smile enraged O'Roon; the vision of strong, brown hands and muscular thighs added to his fury.

"Please forgive me, Father," Elena begged. "I am so ashamed, but it was not all my sin. I was forced to do the touching." She tried to swallow her sobs with several sharp breaths.

"But with your silence there was a tacit agreement." O'Roon wanted to slap her tear-stained cheek, wanted to jar her from the misguided self-pity that clouded her judgment.

"I did not want to do such things. He would force my hand to him."

"And when he finally demanded intercourse you refused him?"

"I tried, Father."

"And how was he supposed to understand this — this 'trying' — was a refusal when you had already let him touch you? When you had allowed this series of disgusting events to occur?"

"Please forgive me, Father." Her weeping fluttered with the ragged edges of shame. "I was too distressed to tell anyone."

"This is an evil chain you started, Elena." He spoke her name without thinking. "I have told you to stay away from the boys, and you have said, 'Yes, Father. Of course, Father,'" O'Roon mimicked. "You have betrayed me every time you came to confession and concealed your own debased acts. You have listened so piously to my advice on such things and all the time you were mocking my counsel."

"That is not true, Father. That is not fair."

"Not fair! Not fair! You have the nerve to bring up fairness." He rose to his feet so quickly that the confessional seemed suddenly unbalanced, as if it could topple over. O'Roon reached out to steady himself before he continued.

"Tell me, my girl. We just talked about the Sansome boy. Have I not pointed out the way you cavort when he comes to the sacristy to deliver the bread? And just today, as you confessed, I saw you brush your breasts against his arm when you leaned over to take the package from him. I suppose that was fair? Or perhaps you thought I was blind to such flirtation?"

There was no answer, just her steady sobs ripping through the silent church.

"It is not that way, Father. Please." Her voice was desperate as she tried to hush it back to a whisper.

"So it was not that way." He echoed her tone once again. "I have devoted many hours to teaching you, Elena, to explaining that you could have more than this." He gestured into the darkness, taking in the town with its rows of shabby buildings. "And this is how you thank me? By allowing a shiftless delivery boy to stroke you. By giving in to his depraved demand for sex?"

He strode out of the confessional, ripping part of the curtain from its hooks as he went. The small brass crucifix clattered to the floor, but O'Roon did not bother to pick it up. His only thought was to flee. He would have stormed from the church, but the taut muscle in his leg made him stumble. It was Elena's hand that steadied him.

"Please," she cried. "You must listen, Father. Wait." She drew another shivered breath. "Please sit." She motioned toward a pew and knelt down beside him.

"The man, Father, was not Tomas. It was my father." She stopped for a moment, trying to curb her tears. "When he is drinking he sometimes mistakes me for my mother."

In the dark shadows, O'Roon saw a resemblance he had never recognized before. The downturn of mouth, the defeated slump of shoulders.

Elena stood up abruptly and looked away from him as she recited the rest.

"Last night he caught me in the bath. I have been careful to avoid him. I thought he was asleep. He said if I ever told he would start on my sister. Father, she is so young. At least I am old enough to understand." Her voice capped the secret in a barely audible whisper. "I supposed he did not mean it. He had been at the bar earlier in the evening."

"So it was not Sansome." O'Roon spoke wearily. "Forgive me, Elena." He stood up, and the girl backed one step away. "You see, I was sure . . . ." He bent to knead his knee, as if the massaging would cure the injury of age. "Your father." He shook his head wearily and motioned her toward the confessional. "Please. We must finish. It is getting late."

"I have nothing more to confess, Father." Now she sounded like her mother, the listless voice, the ruffle of anger trailing on the edges of her words.

O'Roon took another step toward the booth. He touched her arm. "Please, Elena." He nodded toward the confessional. "For me?"

For an instant, she seemed to pull toward the door of the church; but then, head down, she followed him back to the cubicle.

After they were both settled, O'Roon coughed lightly. "It is I who must confess, Elena. I must admit, before God and Jesus my Savior, that I judged you prematurely. Can you forgive me?"

"Of course, Father. I know you did not mean it. You are my confessor. It is not for me to forgive."

Had he been able to find a steady voice, O'Roon would have found his own words to thank her. Instead, he resorted to the reassuring format of the sacrament. "For penance, you must pray for your father. That is all. Now say the Act of Contrition."

She recited the prayer with the sing-song rhythm of a child, while O'Roon intoned the part assigned to the priest. They ended in the customary manner — a strange duet in which confessor and sinner are locked in separate litanies.

"Amen." Elena ended seconds before O'Roon finished his blessing.

". . . name of the Father, the Son, and the Holy Spirit. Amen." O'Roon's words were more deliberate, each one given its own dark space.

He watched her leave the confessional and waited as she knelt to offer penance. Once she was finished, she stood in front of the statue of Mary. Twice she seemed ready to offer a coin. But twice she took it back. The wavering light of the votive candles threw monstrous shadows on the whitewashed walls.

After she left, O'Roon genuflected stiffly at the altar and wished he would be moved to pray for his own soul, but the stuttering candle flames silenced him. He fished deep into the pocket of his cassock until he found silver. He could not bring himself to look up at the chipped and fading Virgin after he dropped the money in. Instead, he traced the raised letters on the metal box with his finger. "FOR THE POOR," was the inscription. Each letter swelled just enough so he could sense its shape in the darkness.

He locked up and headed for the rectory. It was nearly half past the hour. The evening meal would have started without him, but he knew the glass of sherry would be waiting. On days when he was late, they left it on the counter in the butler's pantry.

Hellcat
Gary Barker

When the REA snaked its lines up Sinking Creek in 1947, Verl Rose stole enough electrical cable and hardware to string power to his new four-seat outhouse.

Even before he added the yellowed light bulb and scratchy Philco radio, Verl's privy was by far the most elegant in all of Caster County. The solid foundation was of creosoted railroad ties, the exterior walls were red brick tar paper, and the roof was sparkling galvanized tin. Inside, Verl pasted up rosebud wallpaper, laid a blue linoleum floor, and installed four hinged pink toilet seats he'd ordered from the Sears & Roebuck wishbook.

Verl was working on a heater, too. Already he had rigged a rotating fan, with a switch that worked off the door to turn it on as you entered and off as you left.

Sometimes, Verl would sit on one of his thrones and study the wishbooks, but most of the time he just sat and stared at the big color poster Paul Skaggs had brought him in 1943. The poster was of a snarling F6F Hellcat, the US Navy's superb little fighter plane, the blunt-nosed hot rod that flew off carrier decks to shoot down over 5,000 Japanese Zeroes in three years of action.

Paul, Orb Skaggs's boy from up on Mauck Ridge, shot down fourteen of those 5,000 Japanese fighters before one of them got lucky and got him. Paul's Hellcat blew up before he could bail out. Paul's body was recovered and shipped home to Kentucky. Orb got Paul's medals after the war, and a letter that told all about how good Paul had been. Paul Skaggs was Verl's hero.

Verl had tried hard to join up in '42, but the army refused

his application for the Air Corps. "Read, hell," Verl had snorted. "What's reading and writing got to do with flying a airplane?" Not even as a mechanic would the army take Verl. He had walked the six miles home from Olive Hill, angry and ashamed, and two weeks later asked Buck Cox, over at the Mauck Ridge store, just what the hell was "mentally deficient" anyhow?

Buck took a chew, spat, and finally allowed as how it must have something to do with the way a feller's hammer hangs, and gave Verl the wheels off an old girl's bicycle which had broken in two in the middle.

To a remote mountain county short on young men, spare parts, and cash, Verl Rose's tinkering was crucial to keeping the old Fords, sawmill engines, radios, and coal trucks going while the war was being fought. In bits and pieces, in payment for his work, Verl had acquired a flathead V-8 Ford engine and transmission, a leather aviator's cap and goggles, a pair of WW I cavalryman's boots, a pair of balsa wood oars, six old shotguns, a pile of scrap metal, and a truckload of planed white oak lumber.

Verl used some of the supplies to build his elegant outhouse, and kept the rest neatly stacked and stored in the barn behind the homeplace. Verl's mother, Lily, staunchly defended Verl from gossipy neighbors who wondered just how a man who never even went to war could have got shell-shocked. Lily also encouraged Verl's friendship with ten-year-old Benny Lee Skaggs, Paul's youngest brother, grateful that her eccentric son could relate to at least one fairly normal person.

Benny would listen for hours to Verl's worshipful stories about Paul Skaggs, and it was Benny who collected every available scrap of printed information about the Hellcat warplane. "They was over 12,000 built," Benny said with authority. "The Hellcat, it'd outrun, outclimb, and outshoot any other old airplane they ever was. Why, one pilot it says, he shot down fifteen Japs in one fight. All by hisself."

"Paul, he could have done that, too," insisted Verl. "Paul was the best pilot what ever lived."

"Yeah," agreed Benny. "I reckon he was, at that." He sat, pondering. "I wish they was somewhere we could go to see us a Hellcat. I'd give a bunch to look at a real one."

Verl searched quietly, but couldn't locate a live Hellcat. "They couldn't even land one in these parts if we was to get one," he grumbled. For two more weeks Verl studied it over, then made his announcement. "Benny, I aim to build us one."

"Build us one what?" asked Benny.

"A airplane," said Verl. "A Hellcat. Just like the one Paul flew."

Benny stared suspiciously at his friend. "You don't know how to build no airplane, Verl," Benny finally said. He waited. "Do you?"

Verl beamed. "I got parts, ain't I? I got a picture to go by, don't I? Are you gonna help or ain't you?"

"I ain't so sure," said Benny. "Where you going to put it?"

Verl grandly pointed. "Right yonder," he said. "Right up in the top of that big old oak tree."

Two days later Caster County deputy sheriff Will Davis eased his dusty Ford coupe off to the side of Sinking Creek Road and crawled out laughing. "What are you up to this time, Verl?" he yelled.

Verl, from thirty feet up into the roadside oak, yelled back. "It ain't none of your business, Will. But, if it was, I'd tell you I was up in here building me a airplane."

Will peered up at the tree top, being rapidly leveled out by Verl's busy saw, and at the homemade ladder nailed to the tree trunk. "Lord have mercy," sighed Will. "This time I reckon Verl has gone plumb crazy." Will climbed up cautiously, and was surprised to look up and see Benny Skaggs grinning down at him. "Not you, too, Benny," groaned Will. "Look here, Verl Rose. It's one damned thing if you want to fall out of this tree and break your own fool neck, but you ain't got no business dragging a boy up here."

"Verl never drug me nowheres," protested Benny. "I'm helping. And when we get it ready to go I'll be the co-pilot."

Will sighed, shook his head, climbed down and drove back to the courthouse. His laughing report sent scores of vehicles up Sinking Creek during the next two weeks, and there were daily courthouse-steps summaries of Verl's progress.

The Hellcat was taking shape.

Verl carefully built the frame from steamed and bent hickory, braced by sturdy white oak, and even the distinctive folding wings were made functional by two pairs of iron barn door hinges on each side. But, before he added the final outer cover, Verl rigged a block and tackle.

"What now?" wondered Will Davis.

Verl and Benny sweated and struggled, loaded the Ford V-8 motor and transmission onto a low sled and borrowed Lester Whitt's mule team to drag the load into place just under the oak tree.

"Surely," pleaded Will, "you ain't going to try that."

Verl nodded stubbornly.

Will swore, shrugged, spat on his hands, and threw his two hundred pounds into helping pull the chain. The engine inched slowly upward. "You're crazy as hell, Verl," Will gasped. "This whole contraption is going to fall right on top of us."

"No, it ain't," said Verl. "You gonna talk, or work?"

To Will's relief, the platform held the engine and transmission without a quiver.

"Solid as a rock," beamed Verl. He toyed with the long gearshift lever which stuck up from the transmission case. "When we get done," Verl said proudly, "this here airplane is going to look exactly like the one Paul flew in the war."

Next, Verl rigged a short drive shaft and a hand-operated clutch, brought up a gas can and an old battery, and started up the coughing old engine. "We need us a muffler," Verl yelled into Benny's ear.

"That ain't the half of what we need," Benny yelled back. "Where's the propeller?"

Verl shut down the rasping engine. "First things first," he announced. Ten feet of well pipe and the muffler from a wrecked Reo truck quieted the motor. "Now," said Verl, "we'll get us that propeller." He retrieved a pair of double-bladed oars from the barn loft, and grinned at Benny. "With a little fixing, these here will do just fine."

Before dark, Verl had finished mounting his new four-bladed propeller. He connected the driveshaft. "Will that really work?" asked Benny.

"Stand back," ordered Verl proudly, "and I'll show you." He started the motor, engaged the clutch, shifted to bulldog low, and gently opened the throttle as he released the clutch. The propeller shuddered and started to turn. Will opened up the throttle.

"It works!" Benny yelled happily. "It's going, Verl."

Verl wiped his hands and grinned. "Told you it would," he said modestly.

As they washed up in the rain barrel, Verl explained the

workings of gears and drive shafts. "We can run her in low gear and the propeller, it'll go slow. We shift her up, she'll go faster." Verl winked. "If we ever hit high gear, Benny, that thing'll take off and fly right across the ridge yonder."

"Yeah," whispered Benny. "We can fly our Hellcat to Ashland and back."

The next day Verl and Benny nailed on the thin outer boards and mounted the old bicycle wheels. The Hellcat looked even more real than they had dared dream. "Durn," Benny said admiringly. "It looks like it's really flying, Verl."

"Swooping right down at the road," cackled Verl, "diving down to shoot up anything what comes up this here hill." He smiled vaguely. "One thing we ain't put in yet, Benny, is the guns."

"That's 'cause we ain't got any guns," Benny said absently, staring up at the Hellcat. "God, Verl, she sure is pretty."

"We got guns," Verl muttered to himself.

When Benny arrived the next morning, Verl was already up in the Hellcat working. "Looky here," he said proudly. Benny stared. Six rusted .12 gauge shotguns, two of them double-barreled, were mounted — three to each side of the cockpit — linked together on a swivel mount.

Verl giggled as he demonstrated. "Swing 'em up, swing 'em down, go to either side, just like this. And this rod here, it's hooked to ever one of the triggers. You can shoot 'em one at a time or all of 'em at once't." He beamed. "Ain't that something, Benny?"

"Are they real guns?" Benny nervously fingered the control rods. "Will they shoot, Verl?"

"Hellfire yes, they'll shoot!" laughed Verl. "Want me to show you? I brung shells."

"Naw," Benny said quickly. "Let's finish the painting."

They painted the Hellcat bright US Navy blue, and copied insignia from Paul's old poster. "One more thing," Verl said shyly. "Paul's airplane. Didn't he name it 'Bad Bessie'?"

"Yeah," said Benny. "How'd you know that?"

"Me and Paul, we was buddies," beamed Verl. "Paul, he told me about everthing."

They lettered the name across both sides of the Hellcat's nose, then added fourteen red dots. "For fourteen Zeroes," explained Benny. "Paul shot down fourteen of 'em."

Will Davis came that afternoon to admire Bad Bessie, but

his smile faded when he came to the six shotguns. "Them don't work, do they?" Will asked sharply.

Verl cut off Benny. "Heck no, they don't work, Will. Them's old ones I had down at the barn."

"That's okay, then, I guess," said Will. He smiled again. "Just don't you boys get no ideas about hanging a bomb onto this thing." The deputy left chuckling, looking back, shaking his head.

"Why'd you lie to Will about the guns?" Benny demanded as soon as the deputy was out of hearing range.

"Wonder what we could make us a bomb out of?" Verl answered thoughtfully. He grinned at Benny. "It wouldn't be real."

"It'd better not be," said Benny. "Why'd you lie, Verl? About the guns?"

"Aw, old Will would have made us take 'em off if he knowed they'd work," protested Verl. "It wasn't no real lie, Benny. It don't matter."

"Maybe not," Benny said skeptically. "But you better not ever start shooting."

Verl worked most of the night, by lamplight, building his torpedo-shaped bomb. Two sticks of ten-year-old dynamite went into the center. "What Benny don't know won't hurt him none," Verl whispered. He finished mounting the bomb on the plane's belly as the first car of the morning came bouncing up Sinking Creek Road. It was Buck Cox, grinning ear-to-ear.

"By damn, Verl," Buck finally announced, "you've done it. Coming up the hill yonder, that thing looks just like a real fighter plane swooping down at you." He chuckled. "And, a body'd think that bomb on the bottom was the real thing, too."

Traffic picked up. For a week, a string of dusty Fords and Chevys paraded up the hill. Verl's Hellcat drew visitors from as far away as Morehead, and one young newspaper reporter talked Verl into posing in front of the plane wearing his aviator's cap. Benny Skaggs wore Paul's old flight jacket and goggles proudly, and gave detailed technical explanations to anyone who would listen.

The newspaper story drew even larger crowds, and Verl began to fidget. "Sometimes," he said to Benny, "I get the idea that them people is making fun of us."

"Me, too," complained Benny. "I wish they'd just all go away."

Verl's patience wore thinner. Benny stopped coming by altogether, and the steady flow of chuckling gawkers drove Verl to paint signs warning people off. No one paid the least bit of attention.

On the third Sunday, Verl took more direct action. He scrambled angrily up the ladder with a box of no. 6 birdshot, loaded all eight barrels, and snarled as another convoy of cars came laboring up the hill.

First, Verl fired just one gun.

Buckshot spattered off windshields and fenders, and the lead car slid to a stop.

"Git, goddamn you!" squalled Verl. This time he pulled two triggers, and laughed as he reloaded. Cars were trying to back up and turn around; horns were blaring; people were cursing hysterically. "Take this, you sonsabitches!" screamed Verl. All eight barrels thundered at once, shaking the Hellcat and sending the last of the crowd running frantically downhill.

Verl reloaded, but kept a wary eye on the highway. When the coast was clear he scrambled down and ran to the barn. Verl came back wearing his high-topped cavalry boots, aviator's cap and goggles, and an old .32 revolver strapped to his waist.

From Verl's neck streamed a long red silk scarf.

He climbed the ladder with a bubbling, stuttering Rebel yell. The old engine clattered to life, the propeller began to turn, and Verl's shotguns swiveled to cover the battlefront.

Will Davis slammed his brakes when Verl's first round of gunfire shattered his windshield. Will shoved open the door and dived headfirst into the deep ditch. He crawled out covered with sticky mud. "Verl, damn you!" Will bellowed. "Come down out of there!"

Verl swung his guns around to bear on the angry and wet deputy, but held up as Benny Skaggs ran into the field of fire.

"Get down, you little fool!" yelled Will. Benny dived into the ditch.

"Don't you shoot Verl!" Benny shrieked.

"Shoot him?" growled Will. "Hell, son, it's Verl that's trying to do the killing." Will peered up over the edge of the ditch. "What's he doing now?"

The roar of the Hellcat engine was louder, and the propeller was spinning fast.

Benny peeped out. "He's going to fly away," whispered Benny. "Verl's really going to fly."

Will sighed. "You're as crazy as Verl, boy." But he stared at the blur of the Hellcat's propeller. "That thing won't really fly. It won't, will it? Benny?"

"Naw," Benny said nervously. But he watched closer now. "At least I don't think it will."

Verl shoved the clutch and shifted to second gear. The plane shuddered as the propeller picked up speed. Verl shoved the throttle wide open, and the Hellcat struggled against its moorings.

"My God," whispered Will Davis.

The old V-8 was screaming. Verl's scarf, whipped by the propeller wash, flew back from his clenched teeth and tear-streaked face.

Then Verl smiled and shifted to high gear.

The propeller shrieked.

Then there was a sudden, sharp crackle as Verl's blue Hellcat broke free from the oak tree's limbs. The stubby fighter plane leapt out into space, rattled and bellowed, dipped hard to the left and nose-dived, pieces of hickory and oak streaming behind.

Bad Bessie slammed nose-first into Caster County's most elegant outhouse.

Two ancient sticks of dynamite exploded. There was a blinding flash, a muffled roar, and a shower of hot splinters and metal shards.

Will Davis crawled weakly up out of the ditch and stared. "What happened?" he whispered. "What in the name of God just happened?"

"It flew!" Benny scrambled up, trembling. "The Hellcat flew," he repeated. "Verl's airplane really did fly."

Fire crackled through dried oak and hickory timbers.

"The poor soul," whispered Will. "Poor old Verl."

"No." Benny tugged at Will's sleeve. "Don't you say that."

"What?" Will put a strong arm around Benny's frail shoulders. "Easy, son. They ain't a thing we can do for Verl now."

"We don't have to do nothing for him." Benny was smiling, beaming through a stream of tears. "Verl done it already. Don't you see? Verl finally got to fly a Hellcat."

Benny was almost strutting now, his chest thrust out proudly.

Will shook his head.

Smoke curled up from the wreckage, and drifted slowly down toward Sinking Creek. Benny Skaggs suddenly stopped, snapped to attention, and threw a crisp, military salute to mad Verl and Bad Bessie.

Descent from Avernus
Chris Beyers

As the somberly polished coffin was at last lowered into its earthly haven, Mr. Medwin bit his lower lip and winced, half expecting the strident whine of his late wife to issue forth (slightly muffled, of course) from behind the coffin lid: first, to proclaim her miraculous recovery from a brain tumor, and, second, to inquire pointedly as to the whereabouts of her lazy and ungrateful husband who, with his usual lack of attention to detail, had inadvertently buried her alive. He had made mistakes of this nature before — though naturally, not of this magnitude — and had learned the full implications of the phrase "hell to pay." However, as the last shovelsful of dirt were tamped down, he closed his eyes and sighed, reasonably confident that she had, in fact, perished; or, at least, that the six feet of earth and the thick oak of the coffin would effectively prevent her piercing tenor from ever reaching the biosphere inhabited by humans.

This sigh, combined with the natural basset-houndness of his features created in the eye of Mrs. May Ophia the impression of a man greatly despairing. Mrs. Ophia had been the late Mrs. Medwin's frequent companion — though not, despite Mrs. Ophia's efforts, a *confidante* — in many a church-related activity. With so many years of service under her ample belt, Mrs. Ophia felt no compunction about consoling someone she did not know personally, and thus took Mr. Medwin's arm and murmured, "She's waiting for you in heaven, Mr. Medwin."

Mr. Medwin swallowed. "Waiting? Does that mean we'll be reunited when I die?"

Mrs. Ophia smiled and nodded. "And then you'll be together for all eternity."

Mr. Medwin ran his hand over his face. After its swath, Mrs. Ophia noticed that his eyes had somehow sunk deeper into their sockets. As he absently pulled away from her grasp and shuffled to his car, she shook her head. Such, she mused, is the way with those not strong in the Lord.

The next day, Mr. Medwin took the opportunity of his wife's death to use a (non-accruable) day of leave, puttering around in his house while he considered Mrs. Ophia's words. One thing was clear: Mrs. Ophia was in no way qualified to make such an assertion. A higher authority needed to be consulted, and with that object, he decided to call on Father Eaton, who, Mr. Medwin knew, would likely be in his office composing Sunday's sermon.

As it turned out, instead of searching for a way to temper certain aspects of Paul's Letter to the Ephesians for the modern audience, Father Eaton was searching for a four-letter word meaning Russian mountain that bisected a three-letter word for table scrap. When Mr. Medwin entered, Father Eaton put the puzzle aside. "Excuse me, Father," began Mr. Medwin, "but I need an answer to a theological question."

"Yes?" asked Father Eaton, noting Mr. Medwin's shaking hands.

"Is it true that, when I die, I will be reunited with my wife?"

Now, Father Eaton was a liberal priest, and his views on the afterlife were flavored with a bit of Eastern thought, in that he believed that, upon death, one sheds one's personality and joins with that creative force which Christians term God. Strictly speaking, then, he believed Mr. Medwin would be united, in an indirect way, with his late wife; and, considering the basset-houndness of Mr. Medwin's features and the late Mrs. Medwin's appraisal of her husband's intelligence, Father Eaton judged Mr. Medwin would be confused if confronted by the maze of syllogisms that led to a more sophisticated understanding. In short, Father Eaton nodded, saying, "Of course, Mr. Medwin, one can never be sure God will look as beneficently on Mrs. Medwin as we do. However, I am confident as I can be of anything that God will be merciful to Mrs. Medwin, and that you will have the opportunity to rejoin, provided," he added significantly, "He will look as beneficently upon *your* life."

"And if he does not look as beneficently on me?"

Father Eaton did not think Mr. Medwin capable of appreciating the full implications of absolute nonexistence, neither did he desire to fill Mr. Medwin's head with the terrible construction of hell. "Faith, Mr. Medwin — faith, contrition, and good works," Father Eaton said gravely, "will save any man from such a terrible fate. Concentrate on doing His works and you will one day embrace your departed wife again."

Mr. Medwin thanked Father Eaton and shambled out of the office. Father Eaton knew enough of the workings of grief not to press Mr. Medwin further. Deciding to call on Mr. Medwin on a later date, he reached for the dictionary.

As Mr. Medwin drove home, he turned over in his mind what he had learned. Proceeding from the proposition that on no account did he desire to spend eternity with Mrs. Medwin, he concluded he would have to try, with all his heart, to go to hell.

That night, he worked it out like this: From what he had been given to understand by TV evangelists, if he did not accept Jesus Christ as his personal savior and send them a generous check, he would go to hell. However, he wanted to be sure. The trick, as he saw it, was to choose a path that not only would lead him to the infernal regions, but also one that would afford him pleasure. Thus, Mr. Medwin decided to embark on a life of unrestrained profligacy.

When one has the facial characteristics of, say, a basset hound, society expects one to be the shy retiring type, content with the sedate pleasures of, say, Mendelssohn, hot tea, and the easy chair; the more volatile pleasures of, say, dames, booze, and fast cars, seem to call for a mien more like that of a fennec fox. However, as is generally the case for assumptions about large groups of people, this does not hold true for each particular. More to the point, he had been, at one time, dissolute.

It occurred in the second year of his college career. Looking back, he recalled with particular fondness an incident in which he and his roommate, fired with equal parts half-price whiskey and derring-do, managed to secure no less than seven fire extinguishers from various spots on campus. Thus armed, they recruited two more comrades and conducted a reign of terror upon a cluster of freshmen at the end of the hall that all but matched Robespierre's in ruthlessness, but not, fortunately, in bloodshed. The capper to all this was that, after one freshman managed to break through the line of entrenched sophomores and summon the aid of a pair of indifferent security guards and a torpid resident assistant, Mr. Medwin had the presence of mind to grab a load of books an instant before the rescue team straggled in and appear to be the innocent bystander just returning from the library. The seeming evidence of the books plus his dour appearance was enough to acquit him on the spot.

If asked, Mr. Medwin could go on at considerable length with anecdotes of this nature, every one prefaced with the phrase, "before I met the late Mrs. Medwin." In fact, he spent most of the next day in this pleasant fashion.

As five-thirty rolled around, he asked a number of his office workers if they would care to join him after work for a couple of drinks. The unvarying reply was no, sorry, not tonight, and shouldn't he be thinking about getting home? "Poor Medwin," confided Mr. Carbunkle to the Xerox boy, "drowning his sorrows."

And so, Mr. Medwin set out to lose his soul alone.

His plan was to get roaring drunk and then to bed some young woman — preferably a virgin — and afterwards treat her with the same respect one would a used TV dinner. But, after so many years confined by Mrs. Medwin, he was unsure of the location of the worst dens of iniquity in town. He wandered about until he came to an appropriately squalid place marked by a neon B-A-R and went in.

Where he had hoped to find sailors and other assorted scoundrels with scars, he found only a row of men older than himself propped by their elbows on the bar, watching the news while a jukebox belted out Tony Bennett in mono. The eye of the bartender on him, he ordered a vodka — straight — with a beer chaser and sat down on an empty stool. As he recovered from the effects of locally fermented alcohol decanted from a Russian bottle, the old man next to him said, "I wouldn't drink the vodka if I were you," and spoke continuously for two hours, pausing only to inhale whiskey and sodas or to ensure, by Mr. Medwin's nods and mumbles, that his audience was conscious.

After an hour, it became clear that neither rogues nor corruptible women frequented this bar. However, the drinks had the virtue of being cheap, and so Mr. Medwin decided to maximize the utility of his investment by getting roaring drunk there, and afterwards abusing somebody. Finally, he felt he had achieved his first goal, so he slipped off his stool, shrugged the old man good-bye, and, reeling slightly, left.

In the open air, he had an inspiration — naked dancers! A rather notorious strip of joints advertising "live" dancers was only a few blocks away; surely, he thought happily, sin must lace those places like gin in a debutante's punch.

He was managing a reasonably straight line by the time he reached Jackie's, which claimed to have "The Best Dancers in Town," and had the additional attraction of being the first of such places on the block. He assumed what he thought a rakish air, and opened the door.

"Can I take your order?" the waitress asked in a raspy voice that probably owed much to the cold she'd picked up from wearing the outfit she had on. He ordered a vodka tonic and peered around the room. No scars, no sailors, just a few rows of businessmen staring at a youngish woman gyrating approximately to the beat of blaring Top 40 music. Occasionally, a man would get up and stuff a folded dollar bill into the dancer's garter which, of course, supported no hose. After a while, she was replaced by another woman, who stepped down after a time for a third. Their routines were always the same: They would walk onto the stage wearing some sort of brief outfit, take it off slowly, revolve so that the audience could appreciate their entire physique, and then either redon the outfit or not. The women usually wore at least a slight smile, but he sensed their heart was not in their work. There seemed something vaguely sinful about all this, but it was not to the degree in which he anticipated, and he found little pleasure in it. So, he paid for his drink — four times the price at the previous place — and left.

A bit dejected, he wandered a couple of blocks, kicking the ground absently. Suddenly, a voice said, "Hey, Slim! Do you want to be my boyfriend?"

He looked up. The speaker was a thirtyish woman clad in a yellow tank top, incredibly tight blue pants, and high-heels. She carried a small red purse. Now, had there been a beauty contest in which the only two contestants were this prostitute and the late Mrs. Medwin, Mr. Medwin would have been hard pressed to pick a winner — while the prostitute was endowed more generously up front, Mrs. Medwin was less prominent in the posterior; both women were of medium height, tending to thickness in the legs. Nevertheless, he rejoiced in his heart, for, on his own he had accomplished nothing absolutely damnable in his quest, and here was Sin stalking him! Needless to say, he quickly took her up on her offer.

He asked what was the going rate, and, upon being told, checked his wallet and saw he had more than enough money, a fact the prostitute was able to ascertain also. She said she knew a place where they could go, and he dutifully followed.

She led him down a dark alley and then stopped beside a trash can. "Here?" he asked. She nodded. He fumbled with his belt buckle apprehensively, worrying about the effect of the cold night air on his performance, but tried to reassure himself that he was dealing with a professional here who

—when an intense pain ripped through his stomach, a sear without heat, greater pain than he had ever felt. He screamed and felt a rush of cold air, crashed against a trash can, screamed again, felt a hand go through his pockets, fell to the ground, heard a siren, then high-heels click down the alley, but all he could think of was pain, surprise, pain, pain, and more pain. He crawled out of the alley, and the last thing he remembered was seeing the line of blood he left.

His head was throbbing when he woke up, and the extreme whiteness of the room exacerbated the pain. He realized that he had a hangover. He reflected that he was fortunate that police surveillance in the red light district was heavier than in other sections of town. He wondered at his surroundings.

Presently, a doctor came in. "I see you're awake. You'll be happy to know that your internal organs were undamaged, though you did lose some blood. Your condition was not helped by the amount of alcohol in your bloodstream. Your wallet is on the table next to you. I'll advise the police you're ready to talk." The doctor started for the door. "You are, aren't you?"

"Yes," said Mr. Medwin. As the doctor left the room, Mr. Medwin picked up the wallet and found all the money gone and the credit card folders ripped out. When the detective came, Mr. Medwin said he had been mugged on the way home from a bar. The only things he could remember were the assailant's green coat and moustache.

Sunday morning, Mr. Medwin squinted morosely at the rising sun, his spirits as black as the coffee in his mug. The pain in his stomach reminded him of his own ridiculous inability to commit damnable sins. He decided he needed a more systematic regimen. He went over to the bookcase and pulled out his late wife's thin-leafed Bible in search for prototypes.

Soon enough, he found a character who seemed diabolical enough — a man who extorted his brother's birthright, and then deceived his dying father. Mr. Medwin cringed at having to do things of this nature, which today would likely lead to a lawsuit, but was even more taken aback when he found that, far from being sent to the infernal regions, this man was a patriarch! Well, thought Mr. Medwin, this is going to be harder than I thought.

Fortunately, soon enough he read up to Exodus 20, and found what he needed in The Ten Commandments. "No other gods before me," he read, "No graven image." He'd have to make a trip to the curio shop. "Name in vain," easy enough, Goddammit, he thought with satisfaction. "Honor thy mother and father" — he'd have to write that one off — both those contemptible creatures had, uh, croaked. "Sabbath holy" — well, he was working, sort of, now. He thought about putting in some overtime at work but decided against it.

The next three were tougher. He'd have to kill, commit adultery, and steal. He didn't want to go to prison. He decided to leave those unless absolutely necessary. The ninth, "false witness," would just require him to wait for the opportunity. The tenth now claimed his attention. His neighbors' houses were exactly the same as his; in fact, he considered the house on his left garish, and the one on his right poorly kept up. If anyone would be coveting, it would be his neighbors. "Neighbor's wife" — well, Aberige was divorced, and Franklin's wife was more poorly kept up than his shutters. Nobody had an ox or ass, but Aberige did have a wonderful lawn mower — self-starting, self-mulching, four different settings, changeable blades... Mr. Medwin leaned back in his easy chair, deciding to visit the curio shop a little later, and concentrated on his overwhelming desire to own Aberige's Goddamned lawn mower.

Monday afternoon he received a call from the police, who said that they believed they had apprehended his assailant, and that he should come down to identify him. Delighted at the opportunity to bear false witness, he set off for the police station whistling.

While driving, he rehearsed his lie. He would, with severity and assurance, point to *that* one, the one there, number three, the one with the evil glint in his eye, and then of course sign some paper to that effect while they dragged the man off to prison. Then he supposed he would have to repeat his damnable lie in court, where it would undoubtedly be his tax-paying word against the word of some drifter. It would be too bad, for the other man, but, really, to make an omelet one had to destroy some eggs.

The station was a respectably grimy place, full of joking policemen and half-empty coffee cups. He was escorted to the line-up room, where he peered through the one-way glass at five men — all black, moustached, and slightly pitiful. They did not look friendly. He stared at them, and decided that number four looked the most thievish. Prison would be hard on the man, thought Mr. Medwin, especially considering the fact that he was innocent. Mr. Medwin felt a pain from near where he'd received his wound. He sat down in a nearby chair, still looking at the man's desperate eyes and toned muscles. The fellow would, of course, get a good look at him at the trial, and would not be in prison forever, and likely had relatives. In short, Mr. Medwin failed to name anyone, explaining to the aggravated detective that the suddenness of the attack and the darkness of the alley precluded any positive identification. He shuffled to his car, filled with equal parts of gloom, self-disgust, and relief.

He still had some afternoon left, so he decided he might as well procure a graven image. He stopped by Eastern Imports and bought a suitably grotesque figure, a nasty-looking woman clad in snakes and gold paint, with more than the normal number of arms. The striking sight cheered him up considerably.

He was now faced with the problem of concocting a prayer profane enough to profoundly alienate God. With only a superficial knowledge of heathen ritual, gleaned, for the most part, from Edgar Rice Burroughs and episodes of "Johnny Quest," he was unsure of the particulars, but he felt positive that he needed candles and blood. He had candles, but the closest thing he had to blood was some liver. He opened the freezer and found the organ — never his favorite, probably obtained by his late wife as some sort of chastisement — encased in a coating as near to permafrost as is possible in subarctic climates. He sat it on the counter to thaw, and walked over to the pantry for the candles.

Just then, he heard the doorbell ring. After fetching the candles from behind the cans of beans, he walked to the door and opened it. Father Eaton stood smiling on the stoop. "Good evening, Mr. Medwin," said the priest. "I was in the neighborhood and thought I'd stop in."

The impeti for Father Eaton's visit were, of course, more subtle. First, and surely foremost, he was concerned for the emotional and spiritual well-being of Mr. Medwin. However, it is only honest to note that Father Eaton habitually called on parishioners at five o'clock or so, for, the stipend allotted to him was not generous, and it often did his flock a great honor to extend their hospitality — and, more directly, a free meal — to their priest.

Surprised by the appearance of Father Eaton, Mr. Medwin at once asked him in, only an instant later remembering the icon on the coffee table. Mr. Medwin decided the only thing to do was rush the priest past the living room and into the kitchen. Situating himself in Father Eaton's line of vision, Mr. Medwin asked, "Would you care for some coffee?"

"At this time of day? No, thank you, though I am a bit hungry . . . ."

"Well, I think there's something in the kitchen," said Mr. Medwin, gesturing toward the kitchen while taking care to keep his body between the priest and idol. Father Eaton nodded, and took a step, noticing that Mr. Medwin sidled alongside him. "After you," Father Eaton smiled.

Mr. Medwin blinked. "Ah, yes. Of course." He shifted the candles back and forth in his hands a couple of times, and only then decided to nonchalant it out. "Well, this way," he said in an offhand voice. He stepped in the direction of the kitchen, calling Father Eaton's attention to the picture on the wall opposite the living room. "It's only a copy, of course," explained Mr. Medwin.

Unfortunately, Father Eaton had seen the print many times, and had by chance glanced into the living room. "Oh, Mr. Medwin — is that a statue of Siva I see on your coffee table?"

"Hmm?" Mr. Medwin's pitch was a bit too high.

"Yes, it is." Father Eaton walked over to it. "A fine likeness."

Mr. Medwin had no choice but to act surprised. "Siva? That? I had no idea it was a Siva!"

"Oh yes, it is. One of the Hindu trinity."

"Oh, my!" said Mr. Medwin with spirit. "I'll destroy this graven image right away. The man at the curio shop didn't tell me all this!"

"Oh no — no need to do that. This is a holy image."

Mr. Medwin started. "It is?"

"Certainly. The days of religious wars are over, in our neck of the woods, at least. Each culture appreciates God as it can. While religions differ in the particulars, they agree in their affirmation of a supreme being and their stress on moral action."

Mr. Medwin sat down on the couch, once more defeated. Father Eaton read all of Mr. Medwin's abrupt actions — his hesitation at the door, the offer of coffee at five o'clock, the overreaction upon learning the identity of the statuette — as the symptoms of a mind distracted by grief. He sat down next to Mr. Medwin and said, "Isn't it interesting that all the religions concur in the assertion of an eternal union with God in the afterlife? So geographically separate, and yet so much the same on the really important issues."

Mr. Medwin put his head in his hands and mumbled.

The priest declaimed further, but noticed that as his assurances grew stronger, Mr. Medwin grew deeper in gloom. "And soon you'll begin to feel the workings of His great plan. What you need right now, perhaps, is a good meal."

Mr. Medwin shrugged, got up, and walked to the kitchen, followed by Father Eaton, who continued his peroration on the good effect of faith and victuals until the two reached the kitchen counter. "What's this?" asked Father Eaton.

"Liver," replied Mr. Medwin. "Would you care to stay for dinner?"

Father Eaton eyed the bluish meat. "No, thanks, I must get along," he said, and left shortly thereafter.

After a short meal of sandwiches and soup, Mr. Medwin moped in his easy chair. Idly, he picked up one of his wife's religious magazines and flipped through it, morosely looking at the pictures of happy clean-cut families and an occasional scowling alcoholic. He was just remarking to himself that Godliness seemed to go hand-in-hand with crew neck sweaters when he came across this quotation from St. Mark:

> 25 And when ye stand praying, forgive, if ye have aught against any : that your Father also which is in heaven may forgive you your trespasses.
> 26 But if ye do not forgive, neither will your Father which is in heaven forgive you your trespasses.

He read the passage three times then closed the magazine. He checked it with the Bible to safeguard against typographical errors. It was certain. His heart leapt. Unlike other paths of sin which required changes in his lifestyle, he found he now simply had to go on as before!

How he relished his hate! It is commonly said that one does not hate a person, one hates that person's acts. For Mr. Medwin, in regards to his wife, the two were indivisible. Of course, he mused, it had not always been so. He had once loved Mrs. Medwin — Ruth, he called her then — but the one he loved in college was significantly different from the Xanthippe who, until recently, saw fit to disturb his every moment of reverie.

The *other* Mrs. Medwin (as a convenience, Mr. Medwin designated her M_1) had been a forceful woman. But she had had the redeeming quality of a great faith in Mr. Medwin. The later Mrs. Medwin (M_2, of course) was totally devoid of this quality.

When a man sets down all the traits that make a woman alluring to him, the most compelling is often an equal or greater attraction of that woman towards him. For, every man's secret fear is that the image in the mirror is really, truly, he, and not some misreflection sent down by an evil force. For a certain kind of man, only a woman's acclaim can save him from such damnation.

To be fair, the then-Medwin (who, the M's being used up, Mr. Medwin decided to signify by X_1) was not the same as the present-day Medwin (X_2). No, the X_1 prototype was a bit dreamier. Way back then X_1 had been prone to mercurial fits of emotion, and had mistaken insecurity, glandular urges, and general adolescent angst for artistic impulse. X_1 expected his art — in his case, poetry — to fill the gap between what he wanted and what he got.

This self-absorption began to erode the day X_1 first seriously talked to M_1. At the time, he was drugged by Kafka, and, at a party he attended only so that he could demonstrate a disdain for the proceedings. He found one person actually interested in his blather about meaning in an impersonal world, and more surprisingly, this person was female. She asked to see his poetry, and a relationship blossomed, although X_1 felt inhibited at first because he was not sure he meant all the things he said, and he feared M_1 would come across the same book of criticism that he had.

Those early days made him smile — reading his doggerel *vers libre* at two a.m. and then quoting the two lines of poetry that he knew ("I am old, I am old / I shall wear the bottoms of my trousers rolled"), all the time marveling that not only did M_1 buy all this, but she looked very fine indeed in the sweaters she wore. In order to make the sensation last, on the last week of school he asked M_1 to become his wife.

Interestingly, the more he talked, the less he wrote, the less he spent late hours in the library basement, and the more he daydreamed about smoking a pipe and wearing patches on his elbows. The Byronic fits of daring faded along with the Byronic fits of depression.

Stranger still, how the same event — marriage — can have such an equal and opposite effect on two different people. The symmetry so struck him he decided to express it mathematically. So:

$$X_1 + (MARRIAGE) = X_2$$

and

$$M_1 + (MARRIAGE) = M_2$$

also

$$X_1 < X_2$$

but

$$M_1 > M_2$$

Stranger and stranger. Marriage seemed both a positive and a negative. What had it been in fact?

$$\text{MARRIAGE} = X_1 - X_2$$

and

$$\text{MARRIAGE} = M_1 - M_2$$

Obviously true. Marriage equalled the change in both. To find out how M_2 came about, he decided to solve for her in terms of him.

$$M_2 = M_1 + (X_2 - X_1)$$

He studied the equation for a long time. In the back of his mind, an idea was brewing; without quite knowing why, his mouth went dry and a deep sense of anxiety rolled into his heart. Slowly, he put the equation into words: The late Mrs. Medwin was the sum of the lovable Ruth plus the difference between the adult Medwin and the immature poet Medwin; Mrs. Medwin had changed *because of* and in *the same amount as* his own alteration.

He put his face in his hands and felt a torrent of revelation. For, just as he had needed someone to fill up the hole in his life to end his vain striving, so she had needed somebody striving to fill the hole in her life. She had intended to stoke his ambition with her love; but, the greater she loved and the more she tried to prod him, the less the result. What had seemed to him to be her petty and pointless bickering he now saw in a rush was an intense frustration, the outward signs of unrequited love. While his life had been generally pleasant, punctuated with periodic onslaughts from his wife, her life had been one continuous stream of disappointment. Even after she became active in the church, thereby easing some of the pain, she never gave up trying to resurrect her vision of X_1, the one she loved. Her love was true and unalterable, and doomed as only true love can be.

He sat still, breathing deeply. He took his hands from his face and wiped them on his pants. He was aware of a physical discomfort, something like deep indigestion, but felt something stronger welling up inside him; a feeling, he thought, very much like remorse.

Beach Drums
Marjorie M. Bixler

Lisa takes a shell from her pail and tells me to put it to my ear. Hold it still, she says. This one has a different sound.

I am lying on the sand at the beach. Lisa squats beside me. It's not a good beach for shelling. All we have found are chipped and broken and weathered dull. Fragments like pottery shards from some failed civilization.

"What do you hear now?" I ask. She is holding an iridescent pen shell. She says it sounds like a rainbow.

The trip is a bummer so far, but most of the year has been like that. I brought my niece with me three days ago and now my sister and brother-in-law are delayed another three. My husband won't come down this weekend as planned. Business, he said. I heard music and laughter in the background when he called. And on top of it all, I'm being watched.

"This one has a little plinkling sound," says Lisa. "A tiny golden fish lives inside." Her father will be annoyed that I don't correct her. She is skinny and knobby, a child constructed of Tinker Toys. I look at her sweet face and see my brother-in-law's firm chin and my sister Ann's quiet gray eyes.

She pushes my hat askew and sticks a crusty moon snail against my ear. I listen and smile, but hear nothing more than shouts from other children playing nearby and the surge and crash of waves.

I *think* I'm being watched. Yesterday I saw the sun glint on something — a watchband or binoculars perhaps — in the upstairs window of the house next to ours. Coming down the walk to the beach I move self-consciously, stepping precisely on every other board. I resent those intrusive eyes on my back. Still I wish I hadn't worn this hat that makes me look too much like a frumpy suburban housewife going to a meeting of the garden club.

A man lives in the house, and two children, but I still haven't seen the wife. They are permanent residents apparently. The car in the drive has a South Carolina license plate; a mailbox in front has the name "Salyers," with a tacky picture of a bird like the one on the license. The house is old; it probably was once a fisherman's cottage. At different times in its history it has had additions, one on either side; the seams show and each section has a different style of window, giving it a disjointed look. The only unifying feature is a thick coat of white paint. We should find out from the real estate agent what kind of people live next door before we rent next time.

Our house is located between the beach and Neptune Street. I keep seeing a young man and a girl pass by in a red Toyota truck, the stereo blasting. I can hear heavy drumbeats churning from two or three blocks away, louder, louder, then drowning slowly into the cries of gulls. The two always look happy, and I'm disappointed those times when the truck turns at a corner before it reaches my house, and the music fades too soon. I enjoy seeing the girl, smiling, her hair flowing out the window like a sea nymph's. I imagine they are college students working at one of the hotels or restaurants, swimming and surfing in their time off. I envy them their freedom.

Actually, I'm relieved my husband isn't coming down for the weekend. His trip was to be a token visit in the middle of our stay to show Ann and Justin that he doesn't neglect me. Even that much proved too taxing. Marriage leaves my husband free to do as he pleases. He likes that. I keep a lovely home and appear beside him when appearances count. I'm not expected to sleep with him now. He says I was always so distant; that's his excuse. He's a successful man, and he will have his pick of slender, busty broads at the meetings he's attending.

"I could have warned you before you married," my mother said. You did, I wanted to tell her, every day in every way since my father deserted us. But, at the time, I couldn't listen.

When my father left I didn't miss him. Ann and I hadn't known him very well. He took the car, but we were within walking distance of our piano teacher and school. We had always gone on foot. My mother simply let down the table leaf and removed Father's chair where he had eaten silently except to ask for more. When she slammed the table against the wall, he was out of our lives forever. "It makes more room in here," she said, and forced a watery smile. I could almost count the pulse of the tick under her eye as she turned off the heat under the four chops browning in the skillet. We went out for hamburgers that evening.

Father wrote later asking for a divorce, but that was after a reported sighting of him with another woman, so the request was no surprise. I don't know what happened to the second wife or the third. The fourth wife asked that we come to the funeral. She said he remembered us "fondly." I hardly remembered him at all. It was a stranger in the casket, a face less familiar than Lenin's that we've all seen so often on TV.

My only vacations are something with Ann's family or my mother. Lisa is a lovely child, and I am glad her parents let me borrow her. I am not unhappy, alone here with her, though I've caught myself listening to other people's conversations. And I discreetly watch when I see couples on the beach, holding hands, or three-generation families having fun together, all the grown-ups helping care for the children.

My son Davey is nine, twice Lisa's age. Davey preferred going to camp this year. His father encouraged him, and I gave in, although I worry that he could be slipping away from me. I will pick him up on my way home. Sometimes I fear that he will grow up to be like his father and my father. Ann says she doesn't have to worry about Justin, engrossed as he is in his test tubes and petri dishes, but I noted that she wanted to stay with him these days while Lisa and I are already at the beach.

This afternoon at Lisa's nap time I am lying on my bed at the open window. Again I hear the throbbing drumbeats, and rise up on one elbow in time to catch a glimpse of the red Toyota. I wonder where they are rushing to now.

The fronds of the palmetto tree at the window make a chattering noise in the breeze. It's soothing. I am feeling drowsy when I see Mr. Salyers, dressed in paint-spattered work clothes, attaching a scuffed and dented motor boat to a black pickup. The truck is old, like the house. The lettering on the side says "Wells and Salyers, Heating and Air Conditioning." Obviously, it's not a very prosperous business. The pickup, the boat, the paint-stained jeans — he's that kind, a Carolina cracker. The type that should be zoned out of this area, my husband would say. But he would be amused that such a man is watching me — as if no other kind would. I wonder if Mrs. Salyers knows her husband watches women on the beach.

Suddenly I am jarred by raucous music. The screen door opens, and a girl steps out carrying a boom box. She must be twelve or thirteen years old, I think, and walks with the gawky grace of a flamingo. A boy younger than she glides ahead of her on a skateboard. He is wearing one of the tee shirts that says "Shrimp Happens," with the logo of a seafood market underneath.

Mr. Salyers drops his tool and says something to the girl, pointing to our house and the one on the other side of them. Her narrow shoulders rise and fall; she snaps off the music and leaves, dripping self-pity. The boy brakes the skateboard and kicks it back into the garage. Mr. Salyers is alone again. He leans against the boat with his head down, and I want to say to him: Never mind — we all have times like this. I don't care what my husband would think.

When Lisa and I come in from the beach before dinner, Mr. Salyers is in his yard, watering a young palmetto with a hose. Lisa stares at him, and steps off the boardwalk into a clump of sand burrs. She grabs her foot, whimpering, trying to hold back tears. He is beside her before I can put down our towels and umbrella.

"There, there," he says. "It's all part of life on the seashore." He gently seats her on the walk and removes each burr, counting, "Uh, one, uh, two . . . ."

His hands are callused — the kind of man who dives into his work without thinking of gloves. He is thin and wiry, his leanness accented by an Adam's apple, his hair a rusty brown, sun-bleached to reddish around his face.

When he is finished with the burrs he turns the hose on Lisa's foot and makes her laugh. I thank him profusely.

"Call me Joe," he says. "I'm glad to meet my neighbors."

That word jars a little.

Lisa and I have shrimp for dinner. I foolishly make six for her. She lines them up on her plate, a row of fat pink commas, and gives each a name. After repeated urgings to eat "at least one," she chooses "Elizabeth" and drinks most of her milk. We go out to the beach again.

Joe Salyers is sitting on a palmetto log washed up by the tide, watching a dolphin through his binoculars. He says he watches beautiful things — shore birds, pelicans, shrimp boats working.

"People?" I ask, my annoyance returning.

"Beautiful things," he repeats, intent on adjusting the focus, and I don't know whether to be flattered or not. He is wearing the same stained jeans and grayed white tee shirt, and looks like the kind of man my husband wouldn't want around, not even to clean the furnace. He puts the binoculars in their case and complains that there are too few birds at the beach now, like good shells. "Global warming and pollution — all man's stupidities add up," he says.

I'm surprised he's concerned about such things. "Is Mrs. Salyers coming out this evening?" I ask.

He shrugs and turns to look out to sea, shading his eyes with one hand against the lowering sun. "There is no Mrs. Salyers."

I don't know how to shake him off. We stand around, talking sporadically, while Lisa splashes at the water's edge.

"The coral is dying," he says, and he ticks off other endangered species, two or three I hadn't known existed.

When it is almost dark he walks us back to our house. On the way, he tells me his children were just visiting and had gone back to their mother that afternoon. "I'm jealous of her new husband because of them, not her. I've lost them."

I nod. That can happen to me.

Once when I thought I would leave my husband he threatened to take Davey from me. I know that he can do it. I have nightmares — scenes of a courtroom and a black-robed judge, who will understand my husband's prestige. The attorney will drop hints of my emotional instability, and I will be the parent less fit for custody. But my husband knows I'm a devoted mother. "You'd be smart to leave things as they are," he says with as little emotion as if he were talking about wheat futures. I understand the warning. When he talks to me his face is as hard and cold looking as his steel-gray suits. Davey's happiness is the only interest we have in common.

I know he will never divorce me. When one of his lovers gets ideas about making it a permanent alliance, he can point to Davey and me — he can't bear to hurt us. "Family values." I heard him use those words in a speech to the Rotary Club one time and marveled at the irony.

My father didn't mind when he "lost" Ann and me. I saw my half-sister, the second wife's daughter, at his funeral. We didn't have to ask; we had the same straight eyebrows and dark hair. We spoke to each other as though we had been introduced. At lunch afterwards we talked about our work, movies we'd seen, books we wanted to read. Neither of us mentioned the fragile but indissoluble link that connects us, our much-departed, now finally departed, father. Since then we've sent each other Christmas cards with the promise to meet again sometime.

This morning Joe is collecting driftwood on the beach to make a border around the gaillardias in his yard, and Lisa wants to help. "I should go to the mountains when I have a vacation," he says, "but I can't afford to leave home." The beach is much nicer, I tell him. I find a piece of gnarled and twisted oak to add to his basket.

"I've always lived here in the house my grandfather built before this was a resort area," Joe says. "He worked a shrimp boat. I've had offers to buy my place, but I'm afraid I wouldn't like living anywhere else."

"You mustn't think about it," I say.

"Unless they tax me out, or find some other way to get rid of me."

Lisa spots a ghost crab and runs after it, trying to get closer. It shifts and starts sideways toward its hole. She stops and laughs. "Why does he do that?"

"Survival," Joe says. He discards a piece of driftwood to make room for another. "I guess I've been doing that all my life — going sideways."

Before Ann and Justin arrived I was afraid they would take Lisa from me, but they are tired and glad for us to go on with our established routine. Lisa keeps collecting shells and parts of shells, more than she has stories for. Joe helps us fly the kite Justin brought for her. He knows the winds and tides.

We look for sharks' teeth and wade in tidal pools to catch glimpses of hermit crabs. We take long walks on the beach, sometimes so far Joe has to carry Lisa part way back on his shoulders. I don't know how it happens that he is always with us.

Justin teaches Lisa the name of each kind of shell she brings in. She enjoys matching them with the illustrations in the shell guide. There is *no* tiny golden fish in the whelk shell, he tells her. He's afraid she will grow up to be a Shirley MacLaine. "It got away," she replies complacently. I admire the way she evades him. "Now it lives in a bigger house, a pink shell castle in the coral reef." Justin is the one who contributed the coral reef. I could have warned him, when he was teaching her about that, it would only be grist for her fantasy.

This morning I was awakened when I heard the music, and the girl and young man sped by our house in the red truck. I pulled back the curtain, watching until they disappeared in the mist. Joe was standing below my window signaling me, holding a thermos of coffee in one hand. I dressed quickly and ran down to meet him.

Last evening Joe was watching a pelican resting on a sandbar. He handed the binoculars to me and placed his hand on the small of my back to steady me. His hand was scruffy and warm, and the binoculars dipped and wavered. "Let Lisa try," I told him. But Lisa requested a sand castle.

Joe and I were the engineers. We hollowed out a moat and Lisa carried water, chatting to herself — or us; it's often hard to tell which. We couldn't stop when our castle was finished, and built another with a road joining them. Lisa decorated the walls and turrets with shells. It was beautiful.

"The tide will take it in an hour or so," Joe said, but I didn't want to believe him.

This morning there is no trace, our whole kingdom lost. My hands and knees are chafed from crawling in the salty sand. I remember how last night we bumped heads and sat back on our heels staring at each other. I look at him now and he smiles, his eyes crinkled in that permanent squint. I'm frightened.

My son wrote yesterday from camp. He's having a good time, learning to canoe and making something I can't understand in crafts class. I can see the cowlick in his dark curly hair as he bends over the paper, concentrating hard, holding the pencil too tightly. "I'm remembering to change my socks every day," he writes. "Don't forget to pick me up on Sunday." As if I ever could. I press the letter to my face and kiss it the way I kiss him good-night when he is warm in bed.

We've been here almost two weeks. My husband's image has faded, like my father's. Last night I dreamed of him in a casket, faceless. Still, I'm afraid of him. Sometimes I like to imagine what my life could be like if I hadn't married him, but I can't wish that I didn't have Davey.

Joe asks if he can take us fishing tomorrow and I hesitate. Ann has been worrying about me. She's been making remarks that I am spending too much time with him. We don't seek each other out, I insist, and, anyway, Lisa is always with us. If I told her that I wish I could have my son with me and live in this beach house next to Joe forever, she would be shocked. He isn't like anyone either of us knows at home.

I look at Joe. Lisa has stuck a starfish and a hank of seaweed into the band of his squashed fisherman's hat. He looks like a middle-aged beach bum.

"Snap out of it, you're daydreaming," he says to me. "Are we going fishing?"

He draws a question mark in the sand with a crooked toe, and smiles at Lisa. She drops to her knees, copies it with her forefinger, looks up at me pleadingly. We are going.

Lisa sits between us in the truck cab. It smells of oil and salty dust, and the seats are frayed and saggy. As soon as we pull out of the drive into Neptune Street I hear the drumbeats coming, gaining on us. The girl waves when the red Toyota passes and we all wave at them. I strain forward, wishing we could be caught up and swept along with that exuberant music, but the old truck is sluggish, pulling its load, and we soon fall behind.

We launch our boat from a ramp on the bay and drift with the tide into an inlet. Joe baits our hooks and Lisa is first to catch a fish, but she is horrified at its agonized flopping. She hadn't known before what fishing meant. "It doesn't want to go with us," she screams, and Joe releases it. I am proud of her, that she intuitively understands the inhumanity of dominating another creature.

Joe puts the poles away, and takes us into a tidal creek in the salt marsh. He cuts off the motor so that we can ease up to a mud bank thick with fiddler crabs. Each waves one big claw, like zealous followers of some totalitarian ruler. When Lisa starts waving back they all scurry into holes to wait until we are gone. She has Joe leave the bait for them to eat. It will be a nice surprise, she says, when they come out again.

We are leaving tomorrow. "Vacation's as good as over," Joe said on our way back yesterday. We were quiet the rest of the trip. Lisa was sleepy and warm, sitting in my lap with her head under my chin. I used to hold Davey that way, but he's too big to fit now and thinks he's too grown up. I'll have to remember to be restrained when I pick him up at camp. I can see him waiting for me with his suitcases packed, ready to show me whatever it was he made in crafts. I've been keeping my eyes straight ahead to tomorrow, trying hard not to see anything else.

Justin is directing our packing. Lisa has three buckets of shells — far too many. "You may take home just the whole ones," he says, thinking that limitation will bring them down to manageable size.

She fusses at first but finally agrees, and I volunteer to go with her to the faucet outside to wash and sort them. Joe is weeding around the oleanders, and comes over to talk to us. He is shirtless, his skin shiny with sweat, and I notice a small red scratch on one shoulder. I want to reach over to touch it but I must not. I tell him we're starting our packing.

"Tomorrow . . . ." he says. His voice sounds hollow. "Tonight you and I should do something together. Let's go down to the south end of the beach and watch the meteor showers. I know a place past the houses and lights — a good spot to view them. We'll take blankets and build a fire." He bends over to pick up a piece of wet pen shell Lisa has discarded, one he knows I will like. "Here," he says, placing it in my palm. "Fragments can be beautiful . . . ."

For a second I think I hear the drums, but they change direction and die in the distance. I stare down at the thin streak of rainbow color.

Lisa stops her work, watching us. "She can't have it," she says softly, as if it hurts her, too. "It's not allowed."

I close my eyes as she takes it from my hand and drops it back on the pile we are leaving.

The Terrorist
Pat Carr

I recognized him instantly on the evening news. "That's *my* Mohammed Sherif!"

He was being held for questioning in connection with the car bomb explosion in Lisbon, but he didn't look any older than when he'd sat on the front row watching me with his dark eyes whose pupils weren't discernible in the black irises. It was the same pupilless way he seemed to be gazing from the Portuguese dock, and the only alteration in him I could see was that he wasn't wearing the gold chains or the heavy nugget pendant that crouched in the hollow of his dark throat when he came to class.

He probably spoke the best English in the class, which was composed mostly of Saudis and Syrians and one Chinese student from Peking who also sat on the front row and smiled, which Mohammed Sherif never did.

"I went to school in London for two years," he said, and he scattered British colloquialisms across his papers like English pepper.

Many of the others had also acquired their language skills in European schools, and they delighted in practicing their conversational English in class, happily discussing the merits of Corvettes or the personalities of Lincoln and Robert E. Lee. Mohammed Sherif didn't deign to evaluate either. "I am not interested in your American cars or your American heroes," he said. He always stated his non-participation flatly, without rancor — without any emotion at all actually — but we always knew it was definite. And I allowed him to write comparison papers on opposing strategies for reclaiming the West Bank rather than writing about the similarities between Arabian and southern cooking.

That was the year the university decided that foreign students, no matter how well they spoke English, had to pass a written proficiency exam to get college credit. The exam was to be given twice—and only twice—and every foreign student thus had only two tries before he had to repeat the entire semester. The test, an essay written on one of three topics chosen from a list of twenty that the students were given ahead of time, would be graded by a team of full professors. The classroom teacher — a lowly assistant professor — was expected to accept the panel's decision.

The day of the first test came, and the Saudis, most of whom had a good sense of humor, joked and guessed which topic would be chosen. "The envelope, please," Jamal Al-Amin intoned as I pried open the stapled sheet.

I wrote them on the board amid guffaws. "I tol' you! That was the one I pick!"

Only Mohammed Sherif began to write in unsmiling, unblinking silence.

"You've only got two hours," I reminded the others.

The thin wisp of dictionary pages and the gouge of ballpoints replaced their voices, and they seemed to be flowing, ticking down their outlines the way I'd shown them. I was sure they'd all pass.

I was wrong. Not one of them passed.

The three full professors, in the isolation of their carpets and second-floor windows that overlooked the courtyard fountain, had inscribed three red F's, one each, at the top of every composition.

I tried explaining that the first test was only a trial run, that the second one was what counted, but the three scarlet F's — unanimous in three separate scripts — were too monstrous to be excused, and expressions of stunned despair accompanied the papers as I handed them back. Only Mohammed Sherif accepted the exam without a muscle flicker, dropped it into the slot of his Moroccan leather case, and put the case beneath his chair.

Jamal Al-Amin, an older man who had come at the expense of the Saudi government to earn an engineering degree, was unable to hold back tears, and he brushed them away with his knuckle like a toddler.

"All right," I said. I barely avoided slamming the desk with my palm. "Most of you are scientists. How many of these topics do we have to write ahead of time to be sure we'll have them covered on the next exam? They won't repeat the ones they gave this time."

"Fifteen."

A pause, then, "What you mean?"

"I mean you're going to write on fifteen topics, and I'm going to correct them so there's nothing they can mark wrong." (*Seventeen students with fifteen papers each, my God*, I thought even as I was saying it, but Jamal Al-Amin had stopped wiping his eyes to listen.) "You're going to bring them to the next exam." I looked around. "That is as long as no one says a word to anyone outside this classroom."

There was a slightly shocked silence.

"That is cheating," Mohammed Sherif said calmly.

"Naw. It only practicing," the others piped up quickly, drowning him out. "You crazy," they said to him and turning back to me, nodded their assent.

And so the rest of us began the process of circumventing the proficiency exam. They wrote; I corrected their tenses, supplied the articles and punctuation that both Farsi and Chinese seemed to lack, and helped them search for the words with all the proper connotations. I deliberately left an occasional agreement error for the themes to sound authentic as they wrote and wrote and wrote. Only Mohammed Sherif refused to cooperate.

"I know English," he said. "I do not need to compromise."

But he apparently never said a word about the project outside the class, and when the day of the second, and last, exam arrived, all the others sat with revisions for fifteen topics in their notebooks. They waited uneasily for me to open the choices.

"Write a Cause/Effect Paper on the Relationship of TV Violence to Urban Crime," I chalked on the board.

A myriad of sighs arose behind me. We'd done that one thoroughly. Everyone but Mohammed Sherif had a corrected theme.

I wrote the other two topics. They'd polished those as well.

"Get out fresh paper," I said as blandly as if I belonged to the Princeton Testing Service. "Write in ink. You may use some notes for documentation," I added. That was a euphemism for their finished essays, and they pulled them out with faces as deadpan as accomplished con men.

Mohammed Sherif set to work seriously composing.

I walked between the desks pretending to monitor while they wrote.

As I glanced down at Mohammed Sherif's composition, I could see that his verbs had problems, that his articles were still non-existent. There was no way his essay could pass when the others held so few mistakes and were so far superior.

Some of them copied slowly, but everyone had completed a paper and handed it in within an hour and a half. At last only Sherif and I remained in the room.

"I have almost finished," he said.

I took a deep breath. "Since the testing period lasts for two hours, it would be all right for me to look over what you have and make suggestions as long as we didn't run over the time alotted," I lied.

He gave me a long, steady look.

"All corporations and political committees use consensus papers that are rarely the work of a single author. Even Jefferson's *Declaration of Independence* was polished by the other elected representatives."

His chin inclined slightly as he thought that over.

I didn't wait for a decision and snatched the first two pages of his essay off the desk.

I'd never corrected so quickly or so expertly, and I not only doctored his grammar and periods but arrowed and patched two misplaced paragraphs by the time he'd written his final page.

"I made a few marks on this. It's a little hard to read," I said. "You've got time to recopy it. We don't want it to be disqualified because of messiness." I smiled, but he didn't smile back as he began to rewrite.

I saw with relief that he was incorporating my revisions.

It took a few minutes over the two hours for him to complete the recopying, but neither of us commented on that fact as he gave me the theme.

"I think you'll pass," I said. I knew he would.

He looked at me calmly and I thought he might be going to say "Thank you." But he didn't say anything as he gathered up his gold pen and pencil set, his leather case, and went out.

"Mohammed Sherif is one of the leaders of the hard-line Palestinian group believed to be responsible for both the Lisbon bombing and a Tel Aviv kidnapping last year," the unseen newscaster was explaining. The black obsidian eyes of the young man looked impassively, without compromise, into the camera.

Lawrence and Althea
Chris Holbrook

Althea put her hands on her hips and stretched back as much as the crook in her spine would allow. She undid the loop of seagrass rope that held the gate to the chicken lot. Fanning her bucket of cracked corn at the flock, she stepped inside.

"Here, chick, chick, chick," she called. The chickens clustered about her feet and pecked the splinters of corn from the dust.

The horse weeds behind the chicken lot began to stir, the green stalks shaking as something passed through. Althea saw a flash of white, heard a low sniffling growl and a final, violent rustle of leaves. Then the horse weeds stilled. A few minutes later there was a single, distant yelp.

"Them dogs will be after my chickens," Althea said to herself. The chickens pressed forward as she opened the gate. Some flogged each other when they came against the wire fence.

"Lawrence," she called as she started toward the house, "they'll be after my chickens."

The wind skimmed across the tangled rows of corn and beans in the garden. It fluttered the tomato vines, then rose into the branches of the half-dozen winesap apple trees that stood at the garden's far edge.

Althea picked up her hoe, using it as a cane to plod slowly up the slope to the house. "Lawrence," she called.

She found him in the bedroom, a yellowed sheet pulled over him to his chin, his right arm pressed over his eyes.

"Them dogs are goin' to get ever' one of my chickens," she said. "They're goin' to come in of a nighttime and get ever' solitary one." Althea tapped her hoe against the floor.

"Lawrence," she snapped.

Lawrence moved his arm, turning his head to look at her. "They ain't a bit of danger, Altie," he said. "Them dogs are bluffed of you."

Althea stood for another moment, then turned and walked back through the house, the hoe tapping as she walked. Lawrence heard it clang on the living room floor when she dropped it.

His head spun when he tried to rise. He sat on the edge of the bed to let it clear. He had dreamed so well of shucky beans, of green plantin' and pork as he had loved it long ago that he was almost hungry.

Finally, he rose and walked stiffly into the living room. Althea's hoe lay beside a tiny clump of dirt on the floor. Lawrence leaned on the handle as he took it outside, dry earth flaking from the blade, powdering his shirt with a fine dust.

From the front porch, he could see Althea making her way into the garden. He rested her hoe against a bannister and sat down in his rocker. He watched a line of dark clouds simmer over the eastern ridges. That rain will be good for everything, he thought.

He rocked and watched Althea wade through the waist-high corn. He dozed, and when he woke Althea was standing over him. A packsaddle sting swelled the wrinkled, brown flesh of her elbow. She was sweating and smelled of green corn and tomato vines.

"Something's been into my tomatoes," she said. She had a peck bucket filled with half-ripe tomatoes. All had been eaten at.

"We'll get a rain tonight, Altie," Lawrence said, taking the bucket from her.

"I saw some sign of a muskrat," she said. "It's been diggin' in my tomatoes. That's what it's bound to be."

Lawrence nodded. He ran his hands over the tomatoes, feeling the bites. "I'd say them was more from a terrapin," he said.

"That muskrat's got a hole along the creekbank somewhere," Althea said. "You need to see where you can lay for him."

"My head's swimmin' today," Lawrence replied. "I'm give out already."

"Set and rock," Althea said and went into the house.

After a moment, Lawrence rose and followed her inside.

She was leaning on the sink in the kitchen. "Them winesaps are grown over with worms' nests," she said.

"They ain't goin' to do nothin' with all them water sprouts," Lawrence said.

"Trap that muskrat."

"I'll get my .22 out."

"You can't accomplish nothin' with that pistol," Althea said. "You set them traps."

"I bet I find a terrapin before I find a muskrat," Lawrence said.

Althea grunted.

Lawrence stopped in the bedroom on the way out. He took his pistol from the closet, a long-barreled .22 on a .38 frame. It was not as heavy as it looked, though Lawrence's hand shook with the weight.

The winesaps were covered with worms' nests, almost every limb bound with white webs. Lawrence spat on the first tree, then began pruning the thin green sprouts that cluttered its branches. When he'd cleared the lower limbs, he climbed a little way into the tree. His hand brushed against a nest, and a tiny black worm tumbled out. Lawrence shivered when it struck his face. He slid hastily off the limb just as it began to crack.

"Lawrence," Althea called from the porch, "you trap that muskrat. It's too late in the year to be cuttin' them trees."

"There's too many sprouts," he called back.

"The sap's rose," Althea shouted.

"They ain't goin' to bear," Lawrence called. He ran his hand over the crack he'd made in the limb. "I'm not cuttin' on 'em." He raised his arms and motioned to Althea. "Go back in the house."

Althea moved into the doorway. She watched Lawrence turn and walk around the edge of the garden toward the creek. When she could no longer see him she went back into the kitchen.

Along the edge of the garden by the creek grew a wild blackberry patch, its long purple vines threading their way all along the bank. Lawrence swung the steel traps before him, beating the briars down enough to pass.

He waded into the shallow creek, throwing the traps behind him and crouching to peer beneath a large rock that jutted from the opposite bank. After a moment, he rose and snipped a branch from a small willow with his knife. He trimmed the leaves and knelt to jab beneath the rock.

Something caught.

Lawrence smiled and dragged the turtle into the middle of the creek, its jaws clamped tightly to the stick's point.

"I've got you if it don't thunder," Lawrence said. He took his .22 from his back pocket, cocked the hammer and sighted along his arm.

The willow stick snapped in the turtle's mouth. Lawrence slowly lowered the gun.

The turtle sat as motionless as a stone, its head craned upward, a splinter of the stick still in its mouth.

Lawrence flipped it onto its back. Then he settled himself on the sand. He stretched out his legs and lay back with his arms behind his head.

He dozed, dreaming the sound of creek water and of wind rippling the tree leaves. Somewhere a crow cawed. A june bug rose on buzzing wings. Distantly, Lawrence was aware of the sound of his own snoring and, mixed with it, the sound of brush moving at his back.

He rose, half-full of sleep, and turned, the .22 already finding his hand.

The dog was an albino, its skull big like a shepherd's, but the body too small, the legs too frail, the ears too much like a hound's.

Lawrence raised the .22 and fired, the bullet crashing through the blackberry patch at the dog's back.

The dog startled and scurried back into the thicket. Halfway through, it stopped and turned to face Lawrence. Then it growled and paced back to the creek.

Lawrence aimed at its head and fired. This time the bullet splattered the mud between its forepaws. The dog cowered onto its haunches and barked, its voice almost as loud as the .22. Lawrence stepped backward into the creek. He raised the gun again, but the hammer caught on his thumb, and the gun tumbled into the creek.

Slowly, the dog moved around Lawrence, touching its muzzle to his knees, sniffing his crotch. Its sharp ribs fluttered as it breathed. Lawrence backed off another pace. The dog lowered its head and nudged the turtle, growling as its teeth nipped the shell.

The turtle rolled its head and hissed. The dog fastened its jaws on the shell and lifted, creek water dribbling from its muzzle and from the turtle's flailing legs. Holding the turtle firmly in its mouth, the dog trotted across the creek and climbed the bank by the willow tree into the hills.

The clouds in the east were becoming thicker. A cold wind ballooned Althea's dress as she bent to pluck her onions from their bed.

She listened to the cackle of her chickens as she worked, a sound which grew louder and more excited, as if stirred by the fast moving air. She turned and saw the rooster fly wildly from the henhouse, a spatter of blood and down funneling behind him.

Althea dropped the onions. She picked up her hoe and hobbled to the chicken lot. When she swung open the gate, the entire flock leapt upon her, their short wings flapping desperately against her legs.

Althea's heart jumped. She heard the quick pop of Lawrence's .22 coming from the creek. Then she saw the shallow ditch dug in the soft dirt under the chicken wire. She stepped past the rooster, its talons scrambling as if it were alive. "Get!" she shouted, rapping the side of the chicken house with the hoe.

A three-legged English setter cantered out the door. Its yellow fur was tangled with burrs, and its ears hung with the bodies of blood-filled ticks. A brown bantam was in its jaws. Althea swung the hoe at the dog's lean spine and knocked the mangled hindquarters to the ground.

The dog howled as it rolled away, its black lips curving back, its teeth snapping, empty of the bantam. Althea brought the hoe down on its shoulder. The setter rolled away, hopped wide of the flailing hoe, and escaped through the open gate.

Althea paused in the door of the henhouse. There was a clutch of pain in the center of her chest that seemed to tighten each time she drew breath. She shook her head and saw a short-haired terrier crouched beneath one of the roosts.

The dog's head was set on its front paws, its large eyes looking caught. Broken egg shells were strewn across the ground. Yolk stained the dog's muzzle. Althea stumbled forward and chopped with the hoe. The terrier whimpered and scampered out of her way, its short tail curling down, its ears flattening against its head as it ran out the door.

Althea lurched after it, her body pounding with the tight pain in her chest.

Lawrence caught her as she stumbled forward. He slipped his hand around the curve of her back and settled her to the ground. The wind had become colder, the sun dimming behind the dark front of clouds in the east.

"Put my hens up," Althea said. "They've all got loose." There was the mark of a tear down her cheek across a small cut.

Lawrence leaned her against the henhouse and placed his hand on her forehead. The bantam lay next to them, its neck twisted around. Lawrence picked up the carcass and threw it out of sight.

"Just let me rest for a minute," Althea said. Her head was tilted to one shoulder.

"I'm going to help you in the house," Lawrence said.

"Just let me rest," she said, her eyelids flickering.

Lawrence lifted her from the ground. She was a heavy though suddenly pliant weight, like a sack of grain sifting in his hands. He hitched his shoulder beneath her arm and dug his hand into her thick hip. "I'm going to help you," he said, straining to dip and pick up the hoe.

Lawrence moved quietly from the bedroom to the kitchen. His hands shook as he ran cold water from the tap into a cup.

"Lawrence!"

Lawrence hurried back to the bedroom, spilling some of the water as he moved. Althea had risen onto one elbow in the bed. She was grasping the sheet, looking ready to rise.

"Where'd you set them traps?" she demanded.

"It was a terrapin," Lawrence answered.

"Where'd you set them traps?" she repeated. Her eyes were wide, her long gray hair spread wildly around her shoulders.

"I set one by that willow," Lawrence said. He held the cup to her lips. "I set the other one in that runoff ditch from the garden."

Althea drained the cup then fell back in the bed. Lawrence backed slowly from the room. For a while he stood on the porch, watching the storm come in.

Althea called his name from the bedroom. He took a deep breath and went to her.

She was sitting up. "I've got to dust my bean plants," she said.

"It's goin' to rain," Lawrence pleaded.

She fell back in the bed and closed her eyes.

Lawrence stood over her, watching the steady rise and fall of her breast for several minutes. Then he went outside.

The sky was black. He could feel traces of moisture on the wind. The chickens moved about the yard, pecking at the grass.

Althea's hoe leaned against the bannister. Taking it in hand, Lawrence walked quickly down the slope. The corn blades whistled against his body as he stepped into the garden. The bean vines tangled his legs and snapped off as he passed.

He chopped his way through the blackberry patch. The traps were still on the bank where he'd left them. He placed one on the hillside by the willow. He pulled up moss and padded it onto the chain. He scooped up clumps of grass and sprinkled it over the open jaws.

Lightning flashed in the east. A few moments later, thunder sounded. Lawrence found the runoff ditch and placed the other trap.

All the color had left Althea's face. Lawrence leaned over the bed, a drop of moisture falling from his hair to her forehead. She moaned, and Lawrence leaned closer. Her body shuddered, her breast rose against the bed sheet and fell, her breath leaving with a sound like earth sifting slowly into water. Then she was still.

Lawrence placed his hand on her forehead, feeling the heat of her life fade slowly into his palm.

For a moment, he saw her in youth, her hair spread thick and black about her face. He closed his eyes. He lifted his hand, making a tight fist around the moisture and warmth he felt.

He backed slowly from the room and left the house. He sat on the porch steps, his arms hugging his knees as he rocked back and forth. A hen pecked one of the veins in his fist. He opened his hand and pushed her gently away. Lightning flashed again.

It was almost night. Thunder sounded. Lawrence dug his pistol from his pocket. It was still damp from the creek. He stared at the long blue barrel, running his fingers over the hammer and the butt. Then he clicked open the cylinder and spilled the bullets onto the porch.

A long staggering flash rippled the mountains before his eyes. He saw the setter as it limped out of the garden, hobbling cautiously up the slope. Its form burned for that instant, brilliantly close. Lawrence waited out the seconds of darkness, the ghost afterimage of the setter fading into the next lightning flash.

The terrier ran out of the hills behind the henhouse. The other dogs came from the direction of the creek in the next few minutes; a black and tan mixed with something shaggy, a nearly full stock redtick grown old and wild, parts of beagles and shepherds and collies were among the rest, none of them definite.

Lawrence wiped his pistol with the corner of his shirt. He dabbed at the hammer and trigger. The albino was suddenly in his face, snarling, coming up the steps. Lawrence kicked and felt teeth fasten on his leg. He flailed his other foot and found the albino's head. The dog released him. He found his remaining cartridges and fit them shakily into the chamber.

The pack howled as it came into the chickens. Lawrence fired into a bright image of wings and flashing teeth. The sound of the shot went through the wild cackle of the chickens. The bullet hit the terrier's shoulder, tearing a loud hole in its dark fur. Lawrence fired again, saw the black and tan collapse, its skull brightly shattered. He fired twice more, hitting the ground or the trees, but scattering the remaining dogs into the hills.

Lawrence lay the pistol on the step below him. He tasted blood in his mouth where he had bitten his tongue.

He had trouble seeing the tree. He put out his hand and touched the lowest branch, moving along it to the crux and finding the long crack still fresh in the wood. He dipped his paint brush into the bucket of tar and dabbed it along the seam, sealing the white inner bark away. He wrapped a piece of shredded burlap around the blade of Althea's hoe and sprinkled it with kerosene.

A sheet of lightning flashed very close, the thunder crashing immediately. Lawrence saw the albino's lean body, its large head glowing for an instant a few feet from him. In the next flash, it was gone. He found matches in the bib of his overalls. He struck one and lit the strip of burlap. He felt the heat of the torch all along his arm as he raised it into the limbs of the apple tree, touching it to a worm's nest.

He listened to the flame crackle, to the sound of the wind picking up, rising through the leaves, and then the rain.

The Kentucky River
Martin Kent

Mike was standing in his Aunt Mabel's overgrown backyard with his pants and underwear down around his ankles. Two hours before that, he had swallowed a small, black pill that Billy Carpenter sold him for two dollars, telling him it was black mescaline. Mike wasn't sure if the pill was mescaline or not, and he had intended to save it for the ZZ Top concert next week, but he had been drinking whiskey throughout the night, Jack Daniels, then he had borrowed a couple of his aunt's diet pills from the bottle in the bathroom. All of this had cooperated to produce a mighty buzz behind his eyes, but in a couple of hours the buzz was wearing thin and it occurred to him, why wait? And he did the mescaline. He had been sitting, vaguely nauseated, in a lawn chair and wondering if he would actually see the hog weeds growing. Then he was aware that he needed to take a dump and he stood up, and he wasn't sure just why he did it but he shit all over himself.

Now he was confused. Should he leave his pants lying there? He had yanked them down to try to crap on the ground, but his bowels had let go too suddenly. By the time he got his pants down, it was finished. Now, should he pull them back up and get even filthier? He decided to leave them lying there and go in the house and take a shower. He bent forward to take off his shoes and fell on his face. Mike grunted and whined and thrashed to keep his soiled clothes away from his body. He got his shoes off and his pants off his ankles and stood up, to find that his shirt was stained. He pulled it over his head and threw it to the ground beside his pants.

The screen in his aunt's back door was rusty and torn. Mike pushed through the door and it slammed with a snap behind him. His aunt was watching TV upstairs and didn't hear him come in. She didn't pay much attention to Mike's comings and goings, anyway.

Mike went into the bathroom and got into the shower without even closing the bathroom door. The toilet stank of sour urine because the drain was clogged, and Mike and his aunt hadn't been able to flush it for three days.

He turned on the water too cold at first, and then the warm caught up to it. He scrubbed himself the best he could with soap and bare hands because his vision was now too scattered from the black pill to bother looking through the shelves for a washcloth. The drug was kicking in strongly now and Mike felt very good, spaced comfortably, very awake. He found that he suddenly did not like the wallpaper at all, which was white with black French poodles distributed all over it, though he'd never even noticed it before. He scrubbed and scrubbed and became aware that he was cold; he felt like he was freezing. He had run out all the hot water, he realized. He stepped out of the shower but didn't think at all of turning it off.

He felt as if he were moving away from himself. He stood for a few moments beside the shower, shivering, until the chill had passed. Mike became aware of his heart beating. He felt it beating very fast and became frightened. Then he felt that the best thing to do was go outside, but he couldn't find in which direction he should go. The inside of the house was small and he had to get away from those black dogs, and the bathroom was a terribly small place for him to be and he thought he felt his heart wasn't beating right. He closed his eyes and opened them, squinted, and still couldn't see well. He stumbled out of the bathroom. There was sunlight pouring through the windows in the kitchen and that helped him find his way to the back door. He pushed the screen door open and walked out and stood in the sunlight on the concrete slab that served as a back porch. He found that he could see a little clearer, but the bright light was making him sick to his stomach and he still felt like his heart wasn't beating right.

"I've got to get to the hospital," he said aloud.

Doug Henry was walking across the road on this early June afternoon on his way to the bank, with two twenty-dollar bills that he took from his cash register at the garage. He meant to get some nickels and dimes for the change return on his Pepsi machine. He was wearing blue work pants and shirt that were stained with grease, and a cap with a picture of an angry wildcat on the front, above the visor.

All of a sudden, down the road a bit, someone was blowing their horn like crazy. Doug was hot and sweaty and didn't feel friendly, and he swung around grudgingly to wave to whichever of his neighbors or customers was hailing him.

And got a surprise. A car, belonging to no one Doug knew, was idling along the street. A man wearing a tie sat behind the wheel, with the window rolled down, talking at Mike Cornish, who was striding along up the street towards Doug, completely naked. Mike was breathing heavily, walking fast, trying to ignore the man in the car.

Doug stood amazed, overwhelmed by disgust and disbelief, in the center of the road.

After gaping for a few seconds, Doug shouted, "Mike! Get back in the house!"

Mike looked at Doug for half a second and kept walking.

"Listen to me! You know you can't be out here like this!"

Mike stopped. "Why not? Who says? There ain't no law against it! I'm gonna do whatever I want to do and you ain't gonna tell me what to do. Leave me alone."

The man in the car looked at Doug and shook his head. He raised up in the seat and leaned out the window a bit and shouted, "You can't talk to him! He's out of his head!" He lowered himself back in the seat and drove away.

Mike wasn't thinking about his heartbeat anymore. The great fear he had felt passed when he came outside. In its place, he felt a need to be moving, walking somewhere. He hadn't realized that he was walking up the street naked until the man in the car started blowing his horn and telling him to get inside. Right at the moment, Mike really did believe he had the right to walk up the street naked. He felt no sense of shame.

Judith Martin was working lane one at the Clement's Ridge Deposit Bank. Doug Henry ran through the front door of the bank.

"Judy! You need to call the police!" he shouted.

"What's going on?" she asked. Judy was startled and starting to turn scared because Doug was known to be a sober and quiet type of person. It wouldn't be like him to be playing some outlandish joke, certainly not in the bank. She was already picking up the phone.

Before Doug could answer her, William Bently, the president of the bank, had come out of his office. "What's wrong, Doug?"

"Bill, listen, Mabel Shelton's nephew is out there standing on the side of the road without a stitch of clothes on. I reckon he's on dope."

Bently ran to the front door of the bank as Judith began dialing the phone. One of the other tellers started to go to the front door and thought better of it, returning red-faced to her paperwork. The other girls giggled at her as Doug continued, joining Bently at the front door. "I tried to tell him to get in the house, but he's crazy, talking out of his head."

The two of them peered out the window. There he stood, 350 pounds, five feet tall, naked as a newborn, white as a fish belly. Mike Shelton stood on the shoulder of U.S. 96, looking up and down the road, like maybe he wanted a ride somewhere. He looked at the bank. Bill and Doug flinched back, hoping he wouldn't see them, but he did. He started walking to the bank. Bill uttered, "Oh God." He turned around. Judy was on the phone. "Tell 'em to hurry up, Judy. He's coming in here."

Mike grabbed the door handle and pulled the door open about a foot. Bill and Doug hurdled forward together and grabbed the inside handle and began to pull it closed. But Mike's weight and the momentum he had gained gave him the advantage. Bill and Doug lost their balance and tripped over one another. Both men tumbled out the doorway while Mike stepped between them into the bank.

Doug was up first and threw his arms around Mike from behind. "Mike, where are you going?" he said.

Mike shouted, "Leave me alone! I want to cash a check."

"Mike, you can't come in here like that."

"Leave me alone!"

Mike shoved Doug away by shrugging his shoulders.

He came to the counter where Judy was working and placed his arms on the counter. He moved as though he would climb over, the tip of his tongue stuck out the corner of his mouth.

Judy screamed, "Stay away from me!" The phone was still in her hand, a voice squawking from the earpiece.

Doug, standing at Mike's shoulder, said, "Mike, you know you can't go back there!"

Mike shouted, "Why not?"

"Nobody is allowed to go behind the counter in the bank, Mike. You know that. Everybody knows that."

Two state police officers were on their lunch break only a mile away at the Druther's on the other side of town when the radio call came. The dispatcher outlined the situation for them. They stared at each other for a second before taking off. In less than three minutes from the time Judy called the emergency police number, two cruisers rolled into the parking lot, blue lights flashing. The troopers ran in the front door of the bank with their pistols drawn. When they saw that Mike was, indeed, absolutely naked, just like the dispatcher had said, they both snapped their revolvers back into their holsters. Mike didn't have any place to hide a gun.

Mike was still standing in front of Judy's lane. She was screaming in his face, crying, her hands in front of her mouth. Bill Bently had given up the idea of having any control over the situation and was sitting in a chair to the left of the door. Bill, who'd had open heart surgery the year before, was finding this incident just a little too taxing. Doug was still standing beside Mike trying to talk to him.

The two officers handcuffed Mike and led him out of the bank. He went quietly, not willing to fight with the police.

Mike was taken to the Jennings County courthouse. Officer Robert Hopkins, the senior of the two policemen, went in to see Mattie Ross, the jailor, to get Mike a jumpsuit so that he wouldn't have to walk through the courthouse naked. Mattie had already heard about the incident over her scanner. She met Bob at the door.

"Bob, listen, I ain't got a suit here that'll fit that boy. I called Mabel; one of you run over there. She's got the clothes ready for him."

Hopkins went and got the clothes. Mike dressed in the back of the car. He was becoming sober.

Mike was taken that afternoon to the Kentucky State Mental Institution in Louisville. He remained there for three days, then was taken to the Jennings County jail. His aunt refused to post bail.

After a court appearance, Mike was admitted to the Drug and Alcohol Abuse Center in Louisville. As part of the program, he was asked, along with twelve other new admittees, to write a 250-word essay about himself.

The counselor put it up on the blackboard for them:

Who am I?
What do I believe?
What do I like to do?
What do I intend to do?

Then the counselor, or group leader as she preferred to be called, told them, "Take as long as you need. And write as much as you like; just make sure that it's at least 250 words."

Mike wrote:

> My name is Michael Cornish. I live at Clement's Ridge in Jennings County, Kentucky. I have a brother that gos to college at Eastern. I quit school last year when I turned 16. I live with my Aunt Mabel because my mom don't want me and nobody knows where my father is. He left when I was a baby and nobody has seen him sense then. I don't know what I believe but I do believe in God. I like to party and have a good time. I don't think there is anything wrong with it but some people can't handel it. I like to party with my friends and go to concerts. I have been to concerts by Judas Priest, Van Halen, AC-DC, and some other ones that weren't as good. I don't have a driver's license or a car but I have a lot of good friends that do. I catch a ride with them when ever I want to go somewhere.

Mike stopped writing here and counted his words. Seeing that he was short, he continued on, but this writing business was wearing him out.

> I don't know what I want to do, but I know I would like to be a rock star. I guess I will get a job one of these days. I don't know what it will be. I just want to hang out with my friends and have

fun. I do remember one thing that I believe in.
My aunt told me that the bible says that god is
love. I do believe that. Thats all I can think of
to write.

Two weeks into his stay he left the center, four weeks short of completion, and returned to his aunt's house at Clement's Ridge.

Several miles from town, a green two-room house clung to a steep bank of the Kentucky river. The front of the house sat on the ground. The rear of the house hovered on fifteen-foot poles, set on concrete blocks on the face of the slope below. The house had settled since being built, the rear wall now being a good six inches below the front porch, and now looked as though it was beginning to fall backwards down the hillside to the river.

It was not clear, perhaps had never been known, exactly who owned the land on which the house sat. The tiny shack was inhabited presently by two brothers, who had more or less inherited the residency of the house when their father had moved away three years before.

Before he moved out, he had told them, "Boys, if you all stay here, one morning you're going to find yourselves floating upside down to Carrolltown."

But they had stayed, not out of any great love for the place but out of a lack of any drive to go elsewhere.

One hot evening in early August, Eddie Ratliff, the older of the two brothers, was kneeling in the driveway with a screwdriver, replacing a headlight on his car. His brother, Buster, sat on a plastic five-gallon bucket in the small patch of lawn. Eddie had to keep brushing his hair out of his eyes to see what he was doing.

The two young men were obviously brothers, they had the same narrow nose, the same expression of suspicion constantly confirmed in their eyes. Each of them had scraggly beards that grew in tufts on their cheeks.

Presently, Eddie said, "All right, get in there and try it." Buster disliked the tone his brother took, so he sighed loudly and didn't get up too fast.

Eddie said, "Come on, asshole. You want to go get some beer, don't you?"

That helped Buster overlook the insulting tone, and he

speeded up his step but then something occurred to him.

"Got any money?"

"No, I spent my last five bucks on this headlight. I guess you're broke."

"Yep."

"Well, scratch getting any beer. Are you gonna turn that light on or not, asshole?"

Buster reached in the open window of the car and pulled out the light switch. Eddie watched as only one headlight lit up.

"Goddammit. I bet that old son of a bitch knew that headlight wasn't any good."

Buster asked, "Did he tell you that he'd let you bring it back and get another?"

"Hell, no. He told me that there was no guarantee. Which tells me that the son of a bitch knew that it wasn't any good."

Buster said, "Let's ride up the lookout and see who's up there. Allen'll be up there with a case. C'mon."

Eddie turned suddenly and threw the screwdriver into the lawn, driving the point into the ground so that the tool stood up straight like a Marine at attention. "Goddamn son of a bitch knew that headlight wasn't any good. Five dollars for nothing."

Buster insisted, "If we just ride up to the lookout, we'll be all right. No state boys ever come back here, you know that. We'll be all right."

Eddie said, "Yeah, but I hate to be bumming like that."

"Allen's drank our beer. Lots of times. And you used to buy beer for him all the time, before he turned twenty-one. He won't care."

Eddie was scratching his chin, digging through his beard, considering. Finally, he said, "If you'll go back in the house and find my cap, we'll go."

Buster said, "All right!" and ran across the tiny lawn and onto the porch. He stopped and said, "Where is it?"

Eddie shook his head. "If I knew where it was, I wouldn't need you to find it, dumbass."

Buster turned and rushed through the front door. Eddie opened the driver's door of his car, which swung out with a rusty pop, and sat down behind the steering wheel.

He could hear Buster rummaging around inside the house, knocking things over. Buster's anxiety over not being able to find the cap quickly were irritating Eddie. He punched the horn.

In another minute, Buster came back through the front door with a greasy green cap in his hand.

Eddie said, "No, not that one. My good cap."

Buster threw the cap down on the ground and said, "I ain't your fucking nigger, man."

Eddie said, without any apparent symptoms of anger, "If you don't get back in there and find my cap, I'm gonna kick your ass right here."

Buster made two trips and never was able to find Eddie's cap, but they went down to the lookout anyway.

Eddie backed his rusty blue Maverick out onto the blacktop, and, in a few minutes, they came to a wide spot and pulled off the road. A dirt track roadway led off across a mowed field. Over across the field they could see the silver glints of chrome reflected back at them. When they pulled near, the bottom of the car scraping now and again in the ruts, they saw several cars and pickups lined up, facing west, out over the river. A sheer rock bluff dropped away to the water, 200 feet below. Only a few red streaks remained of the sunset.

A few people stood in groups of two or three among the vehicles, mostly teenagers. Buster said, "There's Allen's truck." Allen's father owned the farm where Buster and Eddie worked from time to time. Allen was a tall, solid-built boy, a leader. He was neither magnanimous nor a bully among his peers, simply the biggest. He was sitting on the tailgate of his truck with his girlfriend, Katrina. Three other boys stood around the rear of the truck, talking and laughing. Someone shouted, "Turn off your lights, dumbass."

Below them, over the bluff, the Kentucky river lay in the night. It turned calmly over gray limestone, over the bones of dinosaurs and over washed-out tree roots, swarming with shad and huge gars, full of teeth and hunger.

Eddie pulled the Maverick off the side of the track away from the river. Eddie and Buster got out of the car and walked over to Allen's truck.

"What's going on, fellers?" Allen said.

"Nothing much," Buster answered.

"Want a beer?"

"Why not?"

Allen had a huge cooler full in the back of his truck.

"Is your all's tobacco ready to cut?"

"It won't be long. Couple of weeks, probably. They're already cutting over around Shelbyville, I hear."

"Yeah, I've heard that, too," said Eddie.

"You going to get up in the barn this year?" This was a matter of some anxiety to Allen. If he couldn't find enough workhands willing to climb up in the barn to hang his father's tobacco crop, Allen would be forced to climb up in the barn and hang, himself, sweat dripping off the end of his nose, back crying like a baby all the while he was doing it, then continuing to cry when he lay down to sleep at night.

Eddie said, "I imagine."

Allen said, "Just like a horse, right? If you fall off you got to get right back on."

"That's right."

Eddie had fallen out of the barn onto a wagon while housing tobacco the previous year and had broken three ribs.

Allen said, "Man! If I fell from the top of the barn, there's no way I'd ever get back up there."

Buster laughed.

Eddie muttered, "Ain't much choice."

Katrina leaned over and whispered in Allen's ear. "Here comes that fat dumbass again."

Katrina's hair was frizzed out, blondish brown. She was quiet and pretty, very much like her mother, who presided over the Clement's Ridge Baptist Church every Sunday morning, controlling the younger members of the congregation with well-timed frowns and sparse smiles. Right now, Katrina was presiding over the bed of the Ford pickup with its enormous tires and dozens of running lights. She sat prim and quiet, only speaking if she wished to display disapproval. "Make him leave, Allen."

Mike was spending the evening making his way from car to car, bumming cigarettes, beers, tokes off joints. He had been punched in the jaw twice tonight, once for making lewd remarks to Katrina.

Jason Kyles, one of the boys standing around the back of Allen's pickup, leaned over to speak in Buster's ear. "Allen busted his head a few minutes ago. Son of a bitch is so fucked up that he probably didn't even know it."

Buster and Eddie knew Mike; everybody did. Mike was

staggering; he seemed to never stop talking.

"He's been doing speed. Listen to him talk, never shuts up," one of the others muttered.

Mike pushed his way into the circle. "Allen!" he shouted; he was breathless, as if he'd been running.

"Allen, give me a ride back to town. I've got to get home, I'm sick."

Allen said, "You ain't gonna puke all over my truck. You definitely need to go home, though. Stupid son of a bitch."

Eddie said, "You got five bucks? I'll run you home."

Mike said, "I'm broke. I'll tell you what though, I've got a Van Halen tape at home, I'll give it to you when we get there."

Eddie said, "Yeah, I bet you do."

Allen said, "You take him home. If you don't get that tape, I'll take it out of his hide."

Eddie said, "Oh, I can take it out of his hide myself."

Eddie had no great desire for the tape, but he knew Allen wanted him to do it. He knew that Allen figured a little puke wouldn't hurt his junky car.

Eddie knew it was best to please the boss.

"Get in here, shit-for-brains."

Mike struggled into the back seat.

The bottom of the car dragged worse than ever in the ruts. Eddie muttered, "Stupid fat asshole."

Mike didn't say anything; he was used to his friends' impatience.

Buster turned around, "If you've got to puke, hang your head out the window."

As they pulled out on the road, Mike lay down on the seat. After a few minutes, Buster said, "He's passed out."

In twenty minutes they pulled into the driveway of Mabel's house. The house was dark, though Mabel's car was in the driveway. They could hear the TV inside turned up loud. Mabel was nearly deaf.

Buster turned around and reached over the seat and shook Mike. "Wake up, dumbass! You're home."

Eddie laughed, "Wake up, Sleeping Beauty!"

Mike didn't move. Buster shook him harder. Mike's arm flopped out, fingertips touching the floorboard.

After a few more seconds of shaking, Buster noticed something. Mike wasn't breathing.

Buster turned back and faced Mike with wide eyes. "This

son of a bitch is *dead*," he said slowly.

"You're crazy!" Eddie got up on his knees, turned backward in the seat, and reached over and grabbed the hair of Mike's head and shook hard. "Wake up, dammit!" Mike's mouth hung open. His eyes were half-opened. He did not wake up.

Buster said, "What are we gonna do?"

Eddie turned back around and put the car in reverse. He backed out into the road and took off, headed back the way they came.

He said, in a voice that was much shakier than usual, "We'll put him in the river. If they find him they'll think he drowned. Allen won't say nothing."

Buster nodded his head and said, "Drive slow, Eddie; we don't want to get pulled over."

In just under twenty minutes they arrived at the dam at Rockwall.

"How are we going to get this heavy son of a bitch down there?"

"We'll do it, don't worry."

They struggled to carry him, but in the end they dragged him, one on each foot, scrabbling through the gravel, bumping Mike's body over the limestone chunks, glancing every now and then apprehensively at the lanterns of fishermen on down the river, to the edge of the drop-off of the lock chamber. They rolled his body in, a ten-foot drop, then laughed hilariously at the great splash his body made when it hit the water.

Mike's body was found the next day, floating facedown below the lock chamber. The autopsy showed that he had died from a heart attack, but the police never found who left him in the river.

Quiet Down, Quiet Down

Michele Moore

Doris twisted her left earplug into place, reached across a small mound of relaxation tapes, clicked off the bedside light, and before her body was between the mismatched sheets, said to herself: *I can't sleep.*

A siren screamed from Frankfort Avenue, the nearest thoroughfare bordering the quiet neighborhood and, next door, Duke began to moan.

Doris put her head under the pillow.

Most dogs bark, but not Duke. He wailed in opposition to the siren, rising as it was falling, and when the siren had died in the distance he continued his mournful solo. He rarely barked.

Doris snapped on the light and picked up a package of her new Quiet Down brand earplugs. "Reduces sound by 29 decibels," she read aloud.

The dog continued his dreadful lament, and Doris felt a slight stab of regret for the day two years before when she had pleaded with Robert in 2-A not to lace Duke's food with poison. Robert had moved a month later, and the man who lived there now never spoke to her.

"Environmental noise at the ear is 92 decibels." *Whose environment*, thought Doris, *Cave Hill Cemetery?*

The package included four earplugs, and Doris was now attempting to put two in her right ear.

On weekends she could compensate for Duke's nightly moaning by sleeping late, as long as the neighbors on the other side of her building, the ones who took care of their property, didn't start up with the whirr and whine of mowers, blowers, and that most infernal of inventions, the Weed Eater.

The previous Saturday morning she'd been awakened by women's voices. Doris had recognized them as Duke's owner and another neighbor. "He ain't good for nothing. Yard's ruined — holes and shit everywhere. It's all he's good for — diggin' and shittin'." Doris had lain still, hoping to hear some good news, like maybe they were moving, or someone had offered them a hundred dollars for Duke and, well, how could they refuse?

Instead, the woman across the fence replied, "Ol' Duke will probably out live us all." Then she laughed in a way that Doris thought must have made her feel like some sort of philosopher. The woman who owned Duke laughed and answered, "He probably will." When the neighbor laughed again, Duke's owner repeated, "Probably will, probably will."

Although Doris suspected the woman of beating Duke, she had never seen it happen. Likewise, she'd never seen the woman pet him or even let him out of the small, fenced-in backyard. He was fed at least once a day, he didn't roam, he didn't bite people, he wasn't skinny, and he had a large dog house. According to the county Animal Control Department, that was enough not to be considered abuse. *Enough?* thought Doris. *Who gets to decide what is enough?*

Doris was staring at the bold-faced red letters specifically warning her not to do what she was doing when a stabbing pain shot through her right ear. The first plug was wedged deep into the her ear canal. She tried pinching after the plug, scenes of the emergency room flashing before her eyes. First, she would call Anita. No. First, she would get the tweezers.

Doris didn't want to call Anita about anything even remotely related to Duke. Anita had said she was going to end up in Our Lady of Peace on account of that dog. Anita had said she didn't know which was worse, listening to Doris complain or the dog moan. Now, because of Duke, Anita refused to stay over on work nights. She saw enough of dogs on her job as she delivered mail. For the past several weeks, Anita had been insisting that Doris talk to Duke's owners. "Otherwise," Anita said, "there's nothing left for you to do but move." Doris would not accept the fact that she would have to suffer moving when the problem was clearly not her fault. She was irritated with Anita for the suggestion.

The tweezers did the trick. Her right ear was clear. A car, its stereo pounding bass, came to a stop a few doors down.

Piercingly clear, the words pushed through her window screens:

> ... So take a switch
> and if you can't get pussy
> just smack the bitch ...

Duke struggled into a higher register to compete. Doris did not like Duke's owner, a woman who seemed to be the only permanent resident in a house graced by an old sofa on the porch and a rusting dryer in the yard with the dog. The woman had a severe smoker's cough and sometimes when she was in the driveway, Doris could hear her straining to clear her throat, a disgusting habit made worse by the fact that she spat — a sound Doris could also hear — after productive bouts of coughing.

She didn't know the woman's name, but Doris guessed she was about her own age — early fifties — by the secure and familiar manner in which she carried her large frame. Even Doris had to admit, she liked a woman who was comfortable with her size. Doris was of the "Jack Spratt" body type. For the better part of thirty years she had pursued the blender concoctions of champions trying to develop a "fuller figure," the kind that she imagined only an eighteen-hour bra could adequately contain.

It was Anita who finally convinced Doris that her body could weigh "whatever" and it wouldn't change a thing between them. The problem with that utter acceptance was that now Doris was left wondering if Anita ever really noticed her appearance at all.

Second to Duke's owner, Doris disliked a family of eight that she referred to as "The Catholics" who lived three doors down. Doris could hear their arguments when they were getting into their car, presumably *en route* to Mass. But Doris could tolerate their sidewalk spats. What she couldn't tolerate was the fact that the woman, with her long straight blond hair and too-small tube tops, had once called Animal Control, complaining that Doris' cat had ruined her flower bed. When the officer came to her door, Doris was so distressed she denied even owning a cat.

Doris herself called Animal Control about every other week. A mere gesture — like scratching after a mosquito bite. When she first moved in, though, she had called every night for two weeks. "All we can do is tell them to quiet him down. But we'll send someone over soon as we can." They always said the same thing, but nothing ever changed. It occurred to Doris that maybe the people next door also denied having an animal.

A plane thundered overhead. In its wake the music stopped, but Duke sounded painfully stuck in his shrill moan. Doris read the concluding statement on the earplug package: "This rating is based on continuous noise and may not indicate the protection attainable against impulsive noise, such as gunfire." She threw the package on the table and reminded herself to remain calm, to "let it go" as the soothing woman's voice on her relaxation tape said.

Thinking about not being able to sleep only makes it more difficult. Doris knew that. But she absolutely *had* to be alert the next day. "The Joint" was coming. Doris worked as a transcriber in Medical Records for the Our Savior Hospital. The Joint was short for Joint Commission of Hospital Accreditation. Without passing their inspection, Our Savior would become ineligible to collect from most insurance companies. The inspection was based almost entirely on the medical records being accurate and up-to-date, meaning that the doctors and therapists stayed behind on their paperwork all year, and then a week before The Joint arrived, filled every line of every form and every cassette tape with summaries of patients' conditions. And the transcribers had to get it all typed and ready for Friday. On Monday, Administration had sent doughnuts to Medical Records. But by Wednesday, Administration was threatening to hold their paychecks if all dictation was not cleared by Thursday at five. Anita said holding checks wasn't legal. "They're only trying to scare you. Even the Post Office knows not to pull shit like that."

I hate that dog. A recurring thought for Doris, along with: *I have to get some sleep.*

Warm milk did not sound appealing; it was already the hottest May on record. So Doris, one earplug in, two out, and otherwise naked, went to the refrigerator for a cold beer. She brought the bottle back to bed and punched on the eleven o'clock news. Then she picked up her phone and punched the digit that automatically dialed Anita's apartment. But Doris hung up before Anita could answer.

She wasn't up to hearing Anita's spiel about why neighbors should talk to one another. "But remember what they told me?" Doris would answer, referring to the morning she had heard the dog making a strange, gasping kind of sound. When she looked out the window, Duke was hanging by his chain on her side of the fence. She'd rushed downstairs to help, but he tried to bite her hand when she touched him. She had run to their back porch, yelling that Duke was choking. "And remember," she'd say, "what they told me, them standing there with plates of something that looked like Spaghettios on white bread. They said, 'We'll see about him when we're done eatin' breakfast.' That's what type they are. Anencephaly it's called. Born without a brain. A-N-E-N . . ." Doris had a habit of spelling medical terms aloud immediately after she used them.

While Doris watched the out-of-focus television change from parades to school closings and chemical leaks, her mind began to drift to the lined column of her checkbook. Rent was due, and her check to Sears was already floating its way through the mail system. Of all weeks not to get paid on time. Besides, with the overtime money, she wanted to put a payment down on a window air conditioner. Doris thought of the pleasant cool air and the noise it would make, maybe even enough to reduce Duke to a plugable level. Then maybe Anita would stay over some on work nights again. Maybe. But maybe their relationship was changing because of reasons having nothing to do with Duke. After all, she knew what The Joint coming meant for Doris. Doris hoped Anita would come over and rub her sore neck muscles at least once while The Joint was in town. After all, she'd rubbed plenty of Ben-Gay on Anita's legs during the Christmas card crunch.

The scene on the television changed to Middle East Desert. The voice-over was male, saying that shepherds in Kuwait were losing hundreds of sheep weekly from the animals stepping on leftover grenades and land mines. Mohammad Hashid was written across the screen's bottom, and Doris remembered when her brother had played a shepherd in the grammar school Christmas pageant. The real-life shepherd was surrounded by grayish-black sheep. In relatively clear English he said, "First the oil fell from the sky and turned our white sheeps this color. Now, they die, like this," and he gestured with his hands as if to say, "poof."

Doris punched off the TV, feeling a new urgency for sleep. She'd made fifteen mistakes on an OR report that morning and the doctor had called the head of Medical Records to complain.

Why didn't he just send it back to me, thought Doris. *I was the one who was going to have to fix it anyway.* Dr. Maffucci was his name. She'd left off the second "c" as her first, and perhaps greatest, mistake.

Doris dreaded transcribing foreign doctors' dictation, though sometimes she enjoyed hearing them pronounce the names of exotic diseases: Von Willebrands Coagulopathy, Guillian-Barre Syndrome, and Aran-Duchenne Atrophy. Her favorite, one she liked so much she'd named her cat after it, was Charcot-Marie-Tooth's Disease, a disease having nothing to do with the mouth.

"Your task is to remain indifferent to my voice," said the woman on the relaxation tape; her speech was pleasingly slow and well-enunciated. Doris adjusted the headphones and turned on her side. "This tape will guide you through a series of . . .

Cytopenia: C-Y-T-O-. . . Phenylketonuria: P-H-E-N-. . . Doris began to hear a stream of men's and women's voices: This 32-year-old white male presents with a lacerated . . . This 77-year-old black female presents with a fractured left humerus . . . . Why was it they always used that phrase, "presents with?" As if the woman brought her left arm in a paper bag to give to the doctor. Doris pictured them: men, women, and children, waiting in emergency rooms and doctors' offices, all sitting in various states of incompleteness, each holding a paper bag to "present" to the doctor. Some with their entire body in a big brown Kroger bag. "Paper or plastic?" a nurse would ask the mother of a newborn in Labor and Delivery.

"Your task is to remain indifferent to my voice . . ."

Doris is standing on the roof of the hospital. When she looks up, sheep begin to fall from the sky. Curls of black wool fill the holes Duke has dug in the street. She covers her head with her arms. Some of them whisper as they pass, "Quiet down, quiet down."

Then she is seated at her desk, headset in place. Anita is there, too, one of the temps. The doctor's voice on Doris' line is foreign and hard to understand. She stops the tape, backs it up, slows it down, and still she cannot make out how to spell his name. She leaves the name off the report and presses the pedal with her foot to advance the tape. "This six-week-old respirator-dependent white lamb presents to the neonatal intensive care unit with her eyes in a lunch box and multiple deformities of all four extremities." But on the word processor's monitor, the letters are all jumbled: JCKTOGK ETOX ANOIG — pages and pages of incoherent letters. Doris' heart begins to race, tachycardia ... she tries to type it for Anita to see, but only random letters appear on her screen. Doris begins to cry. Anita turns to her and says, "Your task is to remain indifferent." But Doris is crying so hard she can't see the green letters on her monitor. Then, instead of a doctor's recorded voice, there is a child screaming. Doris backs the tape up, the scream deepens, turns to a wailing, a familiar wailing, like a donkey gone mad — and Doris is trying to find the letters on the keyboard for this awful sound but she can't even get her fingers to stay in the home position, they're shaking so badly.

Doris woke sobbing, the pillow damp against her cheek. *Must have been a bad one*, she thought, *but at least I was sleeping*. Then Duke reached the full pitch for that particular moan, and Doris rolled over, trying to focus her eyes on the digital clock: 3:06 a.m. The headphones were around her neck. The relaxation tape had automatically reversed to the other side and a man's voice was describing five ways to reduce cholesterol. Doris heard Duke's owner yell out her back door, "Shut the fuck up!" Duke only wailed louder.

I hate that dog. I have to get some sleep. She reached for the phone and punched the digit for Animal Control, but then hung up. *What do they ever do? Nothing.* "We'll send someone over to tell them to quiet him down." Always the same response, but nothing ever changed.

Doris remembered she had asked the woman across the street if Duke kept her awake at night. When she answered no, Doris had chalked it up to yet another benefit of central air conditioning. Now, that conversation hung like a sharp edge in her mind, posing the question, *Am I the only one who can't sleep because of him? Perhaps the only one who hears him at all?*

"Just talk to them," Anita would say.

"No, Anita," Doris imagined herself demanding. "You talk to me! Talk to me about anything besides how I should simply move, or simply get another job ... or simply not worry about that bitch trying to send Charcot-Marie to the pound."

A siren wailed on a distant street, and Duke, who had been momentarily quiet, began to wail all over again.

The clock's sinister red numbers glowed 3:33 a.m. "This is

absurd," she said aloud. "Why can't they hear him?" She stared at the bedside table, strewn with earplugs and relaxation tapes. "I hate recorded voices!" Doris was almost shouting now. And Duke, with his sensitive ears, seemed to hear her and respond as though annoyed. Doris swept her hand across the table top, dumping it all — alarm clock, tape player, tapes, even the lamp — onto the floor.

Charcot-Marie darted from the bedroom and headed for her safe spot behind the refrigerator.

Using her flashlight, Doris found a yellow terry cloth robe, pushed on her glasses, shoved her feet into a pair of fuzzy slippers, and in no time was sitting on the floor in front of the hallway closet, loading the Colt 380 her father had given her way back when she first left home.

"Stuff them in there like sausages," her father had told her. "Make sure all six are facing the right direction, then snap the clip home." And that's just what Doris did.

The alley streetlight stretched inside Duke's yard. As soon as Doris stepped off the wooden staircase into the grass, she heard Duke's chain dragging closer to the fence. He made a snuffling sound, then sneezed like an old man. His chain scraped against his food bowl as he paced, metal on metal. Doris flicked the safety off, pulled the hammer back, and aligned the barrel with his large shaggy head. As she began to pull the trigger her sighting changed to his tail. He was moving. Doris exhaled. Duke stopped for a moment. She wiped her hand on her robe, then raised the pistol again, aiming for the ear that hung flat against his head. He sneezed. Duke would not stand still. He paced along the fence, back and forth like the polar bear Doris had seen at the zoo. As he passed from shadow to light, she saw flashes of gray fur. Duke had the curls of a sheepdog, the nose of a Malamute, and the coloring of an Irish Wolfhound.

Presently, Duke wasn't moaning. In fact, he seemed glad for company. Figuring he would sit still if she did, Doris brought a chaise lounge over from the back porch and unfolded it in the grass. With the safety on and the gun in the pocket of her robe, she made sure the legs were steady and the back fully upright before straddling her way into the chair. Duke let out two quick barks. She cocked the hammer and he quieted down. The repetition of him starting to moan and her cocking the hammer to quiet him was almost amusing.

Sitting in the night air was more refreshing than being in her apartment. Doris pulled the robe close around her legs. "Hey Duke," she whispered toward the fence. "Hey Duke. Duke!" He backed away, then moved his head from side to side and barked loudly. "Shhhhhhh," Doris whispered. "Shhhhhh now. Be a good dog, be a good quiet dog." Duke sneezed and began to pace.

Doris looked up, hoping to see a constellation. Nothing fancy, even the Big Dipper would do. But the sky was too thick with humidity.

When she noticed Duke again he was sitting quietly, staring at her. Doris wondered if she had dozed off. A bird whistled, and another answered back.

Duke pushed his black nose through the fence. Doris waddled her way off the chaise lounge and walked over to him. When she put her hand down, Duke snapped at it. Up close, he was surprisingly cute. Maybe a walk each day would be enough to wear him out. But that would require permission, and that would mean having to actually speak to that disgusting woman.

Doris wanted to reach over the fence and pet him. At that moment a light came on in the house. Doris pressed against the large hackberry tree, afraid they might have seen her. Duke began to moan in his usual manner. Doris heard a man yelling, and perhaps something breaking, but Duke was wailing so loudly she couldn't understand what was said. Then, the back door slammed against the side of the house. "Shut up, Duke," a man snapped. Doris remained still, hiding in the shadows.

The metal gate clanked into place. The man started his truck and revved the engine several times. The headlights came on, and Doris pulled her robe close, praying not to be seen. The truck squealed out of the driveway and up to the stop sign. Doris heard him slam on the brakes, then squeal his tires at all three stop signs between her and Frankfort Avenue. Now, every dog in Crescent Hill was barking. Duke led them all with his donkey-gone-mad moan.

"Shut the fuck up," the woman yelled out the back door. He kept wailing. Doris waited for what seemed like several minutes after the light went off in the house before daring to move from her spot behind the tree. Feeling light-headed, she decided to rest for a moment in the chaise lounge before going upstairs. She pulled the Colt's hammer back and Duke quieted down.

She felt dizzy and heavy all at the same time. She leaned back in the chair, closed her eyes, and concentrated on taking deep breaths. Then, a child's voice called out from in front of her building. The paper boy. She heard the papers landing on the front porches with hardly a pause between the thunks. She opened her eyes. With her chair facing east, Doris saw the sun's first timid push against the haze. She sensed a sort of magnificence in witnessing the dawn that she had not felt since...well, probably the last time she'd seen the sun come up. Whenever that had been.

Duke lay in front of his dog house, facing Doris, his nose resting on his outstretched legs. Doris was indifferent now, suddenly on that wonderful edge of sleep — when it seemed nothing could pull her back.

It was the whine of her alarm clock that shoved her back into consciousness. She could hardly believe the sound carried so clearly into the back yard from her upstairs apartment. Duke heard it as well, and responded immediately.

"Shut up, shut up!" the woman yelled as she stalked across the back yard toward the dog. Duke began a frantic side-to-side shuffle, unable to run toward or away from her because of his tangled chain. "Shut up," the woman yelled again. Then Doris saw the stick, part of an old mop handle, rising above the woman's head. Before Doris could heft herself from the chaise lounge the woman was beating the dog across the face and back, screaming, "Shut up. Shut the fuck up!" This time it was Duke's owner who heard the sound of the hammer being cocked. She hesitated with the stick raised lamely in the air. Doris stood in a braced position, her yellow robe loosely sashed together, the gun aimed unmistakably at her neighbor.

"Well. Shit the bed," was the woman's only response. She dropped the stick. Duke made a snuffling sound, and the back yard became very quiet. The woman's pock-marked face wore the swollen expression of a sleepless night.

All three were quiet. Doris held that perfect silence in her hands, and they were not shaking. Then she lowered her arms to the right just a little, just enough to put all six bullets into the dog's head. Without taking her eyes off the bloody animal, she said, "My name is Doris and I live in 2-B."

The elderly woman in the first floor apartment looked out from behind kitchen curtains that were meant to suggest life on the farm. They had cows and chickens and other animals on them. Doris heard a siren in the distance. On the steps, she wondered if the old woman had heard the shots. Someone had said she was completely deaf, and because of that, Doris had always envied her a little.

Making It Through the Night
Barbara Presnell

It's nearly ten-thirty Saturday night, and Rosajohn wants something, wants it so desperately, she'll do anything to get it, but she's not sure what it is. She has a sweet tooth, not to mention she ran out of beer almost an hour ago, so she's walking to 7-Eleven, maybe to get one of those ice-cream sandwiches with two chocolate chip cookies practically the size of pan lids and ice-cream as thick as a fist. If they still sell those things. She and Sam used to get them when they were living in Virginia. They'd take off walking to 7-Eleven, or whatever they called 'em there, late in the night. Sometimes Sam'd crawl out of bed just because she was wanting one, or more likely he was wanting it and talked her into it. That was before they found out about Sam's cholesterol, before they had to quit eating ice-cream and chocolate, before all they had to get excited about was chicken with the skin pulled off. Sometimes Rosajohn thinks the real reason she and Sam split up was food. So much of their time together was spent eating, beginning with their very first date when they polished off a large pizza with extra cheese and olives. Irreconcilable differences in the bloodstream, she pictures herself saying to the judge. I've got to have red meat. My body needs fat to survive.

The moon is full tonight, or else it's just the streetlight, she can't be sure. Her shadows, three of them, intersecting like geometric circles, play at her feet. As she turns into the parking lot they swing far to her left like a scarf she's tossed over her shoulder. They cling to the side of her shoe until they darken and disappear when she steps into the fluorescent light. She suddenly misses them, hadn't realized she'd counted on them as friends, and plans to hurry out so they won't wander off while she's inside.

Behind the cash register is a middle-aged man. His face is square, his hair wet and combed back from his forehead, he's wearing an orange jacket that says 7-Eleven over the pocket, and he stares at her through dark Tootsie-Roll eyes under brows that make her think of porcupines. She stuffs her hands in her pockets and tosses him a quick smile but doesn't look at him. There's a kid playing a video game in the corner by the freezer. He's propped a cigarette on the windowsill; he stops between plays and takes a long, serious drag while he studies the machine. He looks fourteen. Will that be Joey one day, she quickly wonders, but she wonders that these days whenever she sees a kid. Particularly kids who look like they're from what her mother used to call "broken homes." As though her own living room is split right in two.

She wants something, what is it? She glides up and down the aisles. Something sweet? Something salty? She selects a large bag of Chee-tos — Joey calls them cheese worms — and a half-pounder of M&M's. Sam wouldn't be able to eat either one, and she thinks about that as she picks them off the shelf. She reaches in the cooler and gets a quart of Budweiser. It's been a long time since she's had beer by the quart — since she and Sam were first dating and it seemed like the ultimate romance to drink from the same bottle, like passing kisses back and forth. That was before she learned that over a thousand living organisms can thrive in a single drop of saliva.

She places her items on the counter between a box of whistle-shaped bubble gum and free red and orange 7-Eleven matches.

"Is that all?" He looks up at her with those chocolaty eyes, speaks to her as though he means what he says.

"I think so." But she feels compelled by those eyes to get something else. She fingers the wrapper of a pink and green bubble gum whistle. "Do these really work?"

"Package says they do."

"Well, I'll get one," She says. "I've got a little boy, you know. He'd like it."

He's chewing on something, she notices, probably Juicy Fruit or Dentyne, and snapping his gum like her mother used to when she ironed and listened to Tommy Dorsey records. He rings her purchases.

"He's spending the night with his daddy," Rosajohn says.

"My little boy. We don't live together anymore, his daddy and me."

"That'll be five dollars and forty-three cents."

She digs in her pocket, hands him a bill and two quarters. "I didn't want you to think I'd left him home alone."

She has spent the entire day not talking to a single living human being, not since morning when Sam came over and picked up Joey. For an hour or two she liked being alone — after all, it's her first free Saturday in the six years since Joey was born — but the fun wore off quickly. By afternoon she was on the phone calling all the names in her address book from Roanoke to Modesto, but nobody answered the phone. She even called information for numbers she had just to hear the sound of a voice on the end of the line.

She suddenly gets the urge to pour every thought in her head onto this man like honey on waffles. She doesn't know his name or where he lives or if he has a wife or not. For all she knows he's divorced three women already, or he could be a Baptist deacon, or a rapist. It doesn't matter. All that matters now is that he has eyes that say, "I care."

"It's only been a week so far," she begins, with a fresh lift in her voice that sounds promising even to her. "This is his first night with his daddy. I called 'em up a while ago, and they were having a grand old time — watching basketball. I hate basketball. Do you have kids?"

He hands her a nickel and two pennies, and his fingers touch her palm and seem to hold there. Is he making a pass at her? She pulls her pupils into bull's-eye range with his, and discovers he's looking behind her where the kid from the video game is now standing, holding a crumpled dollar bill.

"Thank you for shopping 7-Eleven," he says at the same time that he takes the bill from the kid.

"Oh, well, you're welcome." She moves a step back, stuffs her change into her pockets and gathers her paper bag. She takes a last glance at the man as he gives the kid a handful of quarters.

She feels an old twinge of regret for losing Sam, and a new one for losing this man behind the cash register. She has almost connected, she thinks, and it almost feels worse than no connection at all. She wishes now she'd gotten some of those ice-cream sandwiches, a box full, but she won't dare go back.

She likes to consider herself an expert on reading people's

eyes, and feels foolish when a set of them tricks her like that. Her daddy, for instance, had eyes that said, "I need you." They'd shine like patent leather shoes, and when she sat beside him on the couch while he read stories to her, she knew it meant more to him than it did to her, so she let him read to her as often as he wanted. That was before he left her and her mother — who didn't like reading out loud — to work in a lumber yard in St. Louis. She was fourteen and hasn't seen him since.

Sometimes she thinks she married Sam because his eyes were just like her daddy's, and for almost ten years she's believed what they've been saying to her. They say something else, though, loud and clear. The left one twitches out of control whenever Sam is lying, and it's gotten so it's twitching all the time. He says to her, "I love you," and that eye just about jumps right out of the socket, twitching just as fast as it can. And if it is twitching that fast with words that are meant to be true, how can she believe what his eyes are saying to her when his voice isn't speaking at all?

It's midnight and Rosajohn has eaten cheese puffs until her hands are stained so yellow that no amount of rubbing with a napkin will clean them. She imagines her mouth must look the same, but she doesn't get up to check it. She eats M&M's one by one, the tan ones first, then brown, then yellow, then red. The green ones she gathers on a plate like lima beans. They've always been Joey's favorite — green M&M's, that is, not lima beans.

Cheese puffs and M&M's have comforted her like an electric blanket, but inside she is still cold with want for something. She kicked off her shoes an hour or so ago when she stretched out on the couch and turned on the TV. Her eyes are fixed on the screen, though if somebody walked in and asked, she couldn't begin to tell what she is watching or who is in it, because she's watching a movie of her own deep inside her head. She ought to go to bed, she thinks, but her eyes don't seem very interested in closing, and the quart of beer, balanced on the rug beside her and more than half-empty now, has given her the freedom to think thoughts that the daytime pushes away.

She's thinking about Sam. First she conjures up a picture of him, as lifelike as if he were standing in her living room. She puts him in a pair of jeans and that yellow tee shirt with the balloon on the back that she's always liked. He's standing there in the room, smiling at her, he's just had his hair cut close and neat, and he looks like a little boy, looks a lot like Joey, but she always has said that. She's missing him, there's no doubt about it, missing him the way she misses taking codeine cough medicine once her cough is gone, missing that heavy, comfortable, giving-in feeling.

She stands suddenly, shakes her head to erase the picture, slaps her face awake, and stretches the muscles in her arms and legs. Maybe she ought to try that Modesto number again, she thinks. It's only nine o'clock out there, and if she could just talk to somebody, anybody, she might make it through till morning.

She shuffles in her socks to her desk drawer, finds her address book. She has just dialed the area code when she hears a tap-tap on the front door. She hears the storm door open and another light tap-tap. She puts down the phone, watches the door. She hears a key slip into the lock, the handle turns slowly, and she's standing there like a piece of furniture when Sam sticks his head in the door. Joey's face is hidden in the dark of Sam's jacket.

"Rosajohn?" He sees her and pushes the door open. Joey is hanging onto his leg, but when the boy sees her, he lets go and races to her. She bends on her knees and grabs his hug.

"I can't get him to sleep," Sam says. He steps all the way in and closes the door. He's carrying Joey's overnight pack, has Joey's blanket draped over his shoulder. He puts the pack down on the floor and the blanket on the kitchen table.

Joey clings to her like plastic wrap, nearly chokes her with his arms. It wasn't Joey she'd been missing, but his tight grip is a sunny day. She stands, pulling up with help from the wall, and brings Joey with her.

"You okay, honey?" She brushes her hand through his hair and feels his head nod.

Sam unzips his jacket. He's wearing that yellow tee shirt. She'd forgotten how worn out it had become, holes around the collar and the front pocket, and faded almost to white. In her picture it was nearly new and bright yellow.

"He's just been crying and sitting by himself. Won't have a thing to do with me," Sam said. "I thought it'd be best to bring him back."

"Well, I'll take him tonight," she says, her voice sounding

tougher than she feels, "but you two are gonna have to work this out."

"We will," Sam says. "I'll see him tomorrow."

Rosajohn doesn't speak for a moment. She feels Joey's breathing warm and steady against her chest, his body relaxing on her arm.

Sam turns to leave. She grabs his wrist, stops him by the door.

"Why don't you stay?" she says, feeling for the second time tonight a sudden clearing, a hope.

"I shouldn't," he says, not looking at her.

"Joey will go to sleep soon," she says. "We could stay up and talk. I've got some beer."

He looks at her, looks at Joey, puts his hand on the doorknob.

"I can't, really," he says.

A smile crosses her face. "You've got some plans?"

"No, of course not." She looks at him and in a brief second it begins, like the slow dripping of a faucet that becomes a stream, that left eye twitching, harder and faster. He wipes his hand across his temple as though he's trying to stop it or hide it, but when he takes his hand away, it's still there, throbbing like a heartbeat.

She shakes her head, lets out a stream of air. "Lord, Sam," is all she can say.

Without speaking, he opens the door, touches Joey briefly on the head, steps out, and is gone. They stand by the door and watch his headlights pop on then move slowly out of the driveway and into the street. Joey leans his head on her shoulder, sucks on his thumb.

"Would you like a glass of milk?" He nods. Her arm is beginning to cramp with his weight, so she sets him on his feet beside her. He holds tight to her leg.

He's wearing red and white ALF pajamas that are a size too large and gathered loosely around his wrists and ankles. She gets two glasses, one for her too, fills them half-full with milk, gives Joey his, sips on hers. He holds his glass with two hands, and as he drinks he peers at her over the edge with the prettiest pair of I-need-you eyes she's ever seen, looking straight at her, wide open and steady as the moon.

She holds out her hand to him, and he takes it.

"I saved you some green M&M's," she says. "Let's get us

a book and sit on the couch and read some while we eat 'em."

He smiles, and she scoops him into her arms, spilling the last drops of his milk onto the kitchen floor. He wraps is arms around her neck once again.

As they walk to the couch, Rosajohn presses her cheek against his hair, and for the third time tonight, begins to feel something good seeping in. It's chancy, she knows, but right now it will see her through till morning.

from "Scenic Roots"
Deborah Reed

JULY 1971

The bombs had missed her. She was still alive. She dragged herself along the edge of the jungle using her elbows for leverage, planning her tombstone as she went. "Youngest Air Force Hero Ever," it would say. "A courageous spy, shot down in the line of duty saving countless women and children."

Since Sonny Boy's last letter, spying had become a nagging confusion. In it he had told her he held our own spies responsible for a lot of innocent people getting murdered, someplace called Da Nang.

All that summer she spied on grown-ups from beneath the front porch, hidden by the white latticework that ran around it all the way down to where the morning glory vines started. Under Miss Helen's bedroom window Molly had removed a section of lattice, taking out the slender, steel nails one by one with the blade of her pocket knife. Then she could crawl undetected through the soft, cool dirt, smooth except for her own track or that of a nocturnal possum, and listen for the answers to questions she had not yet figured out how to ask.

Above her, Miss Helen's yoga teacher was telling a joke about taming the mind. Miss Helen, listening for the punch line, shifted her wicker chair a little closer to the coffee table, picked up her bourbon and water and drained it. Abruptly, she set the tumbler down so hard Molly could hear the glass tabletop crack. Miss Helen laughed her empty cartoon-bubble laugh to cover her astonishment. The yoga teacher sucked air. "Lord, Helen!" she exclaimed in a soft, spiritually bewildered voice. "Breathe," she instructed. The yoga teacher inhaled deeply through her small nose to show how it was done. "Now, ommm, Helen, ommmmmmm."

The yoga teacher had been drinking Hawaiian Punch and eating fig newtons when Miss Helen exploded, "Om, my ass!" and for emphasis shoved the table with the toe of her shoe, causing the glass top to fall out right above Molly's head.

"I think I'd best be going now, Helen," the yoga teacher said. Molly heard her get up from the fat pink pillow she carried with her everywhere. "I'll see you in class, Helen," she said, walking down the steps. Molly watched her cross their yard, wading through lightning bugs as high as her knees, and drive away in the pale green Nash station wagon with her fat pillow on the back seat. Miss Helen went to the kitchen and mixed another drink. She turned on the opera and sat in the living room after the yoga teacher left, so Molly figured she'd crawl out.

In her room she lay on her stomach beneath the four-poster bed and began a letter to Sonny Boy, using a yellow Mallard pencil and her flashlight. She wrote Sonny Boy a lot more now that she was growing up.

July 1, 1971

Dear Sonny Boy,

I have got to tell <u>somebody</u> what I have to deal with here. I know you are very busy with the war, but it's like a war here, too. We have run through three console TVs since you've been gone. I guess I told you about the Huntley-Brinkley boys and our daddy's 12-gauge. Well, the new one was delivered last week. It is walnut and has doors on it that close over the picture tube. Miss Helen says she can't stand to have that big eye following her around the house, so Buffalo got one where you can cover up the eye. It is still sitting against the wall in the living room across from the piano. Buffalo's gone away for I don't know how long and I'm not to bother you about it so he hasn't ordered a new one. Miss Helen said this one is Johnny Carson's fault. He told a joke Wednesday night that she said made women generally, and her in particular, feel like chattel. At first I thought she said cattle but I looked it up. It means property. She was still dressed up from going in town with Georgena and Lilly for beauty parlor day and wearing red high-heel shoes. So that's what was handy when Johnny Carson told his joke. She smacked the new console TV picture with one of those tall heels and it went in like an ice pick. It's still there so the doors won't close over it. Lilly came up yesterday and vacuumed the glass but Miss Helen said for her to leave the shoe — that it ruined the eye for following her around the house. I already told you about the baby turtles that Pud put in the first one so that's three. I think we'll get another one soon cause Miss Helen can't stand to have us underfoot every night.

Lilly went for a walk with Miss Helen while Georgena was still under the drier on beauty parlor day. They came to a big piece of wet cement where there is a Texaco station going in, and Miss Helen took a stick and wrote in the concrete "UP THE ASS OF THE RULING CLASS."

"Who's that, Helen?" Lilly asks. "Men!" says Mama, mad like.

I heard her tell Georgena this before I stopped spying. But I *do* still like to stay under the porch where it's cool. Well, I've got to go now.

Love and kisses,

    OOOXXX   Molly

AUGUST 1971

Her original intention, when she was just a kid, had been to fly, and she had nearly accomplished that by leaping from the smokehouse roof, an enormous orange silk parachute that Sonny Boy had sent her from Vietnam tied around her neck. Not exactly accomplished, maybe, but tested the theory to her satisfaction. She'd bit the least tip of her tongue off when she landed and practically smothered to death before Georgena and Lilly got the parachute from round her head; it is quite a shock to the brain to flatten out on hard dirt when your mind is set on flying.

Now she crouched precariously on top of a wet corner post, testing her ability to win that air by springing a ten-foot span to the roof of the pig house. She felt her feet slide on the rain-soaked locust wood the second she jumped, and she fell gracelessly, her buttocks settling into the deep brown slop of the pig pen in a soft embracing plop. She was wearing Miss Helen's old green rubber raincoat and the hood fell off as she landed, her legs thrust out before her in the direction of the sow and shoat. Disgusted, she sank slowly into the mud, while the hood on her mama's coat filled up with water from the sky and the fresh creeks of her hair.

Boone and Lee Roy and Pud were watching her from the porch, and their voices hee-hawed in fun and malice.

"They don't mean nothin'," she said to herself, and her desire for compassion momentarily overcame reason. Then a fat dirt clod smacked the back of her head and fell into the gaping hood on the raincoat. "Lee Roooy! " she yelled.

Lee Roy was the only one of her brothers who could throw that far and straight at the same time. Boone and Pud threw underhanded, like girls, when Lee Roy wasn't around to tease them. Pud, the baby, still threw for joy. Lee Roy threw to hurt, and sometimes to kill. Last spring Lee Roy got a Red Ryder BB gun for his birthday. Miss Helen said she gave it to him to stop him whining for one, but it was a well-known fact that Miss Helen would give Lee Roy most anything he wanted unless she thought he'd maim himself with it, and with his short arms she felt like he'd be hard-pressed to hold a long-barreled Red Ryder air rifle to his head and shoot himself. She gave him plenty of Quicksilver BBs to go with it, of course, and before the morning was out Lee Roy had shot about a package of BBs into everything on the farm that didn't move. He *had* been warned against things that did.

Molly was watching Lee Roy from an old winesap tree, and she could see clear inside his bored head. Uncle Brother's black Angus bull was grazing in the front pasture by the house, keeping close to the little shade a young maple tree afforded. She saw Lee Roy perk up and pat his BB pocket when he noticed the bull. Uncle Brother'd bought that bull for breeding to the good cows, and he had the biggest, lowest hanging-to-the-ground set of balls Molly had ever seen, and it was those balls that had just caught Lee Roy's attention. Lee Roy crouched down behind a wild rosebush so the bull couldn't see him, raised the gun to his shoulder, aimed an fired one off. Molly thought he probably would have quit with that first shot if the bull hadn't provided such a satisfying show. "UMPH!" huffed the bull, like all the wind'd been knocked out of him and went down on his knees, wide-eyed with shock. After a while he got up, but real slow, looking back over his shoulder toward his balls, puzzling the way any slow thinker will do and trying to figure out what had happened to him. As soon as the bull got readjusted, Lee Roy fired his second shot, and down he went again. "UMPH!" Then the bull repeated the whole process, this time ending up not as well-adjusted as the first time.

Lee Roy emptied the whole package of BBs into the bull's balls that afternoon; when he finished the balls were so heavy they practically dragged the ground, and the skin that held the balls to his belly was stretched tight as pulled taffy. When Uncle Brother got home he went out to see shy the bull wouldn't get up and saw the tiny blue bruises completely covering the balls. He was so agitated he walked through the house to the telephone without bothering to wipe the mud from his boots.

Doc Snyder hurried out with two university men and looked at the bull, and they scratched their heads till well after dark. They never did figure out what disease that bull had, but since he'd been brought up from Baton Rouge the university men thought it might be something tropical. The next morning Uncle Brother had to put him down. So you can understand how Lee Roy is not exactly your normal brother.

Molly sat with her eyes closed in the warm mud, recollecting her throwing arm pulling back and letting go. "One," she counted, "two, three, four, five, six, seven!" Seven skips! Nearly halfway across the Kentucky, a river to be reckoned with. It is something to measure her worth by now, when times are not so good. Seven skips and half way across a reckoning river.

Molly didn't holler when the clod hit, which in her view would have given satisfaction to the audience on the porch.

Instead, she allowed her throwing left hand to suck up from the mud and rub round drip-slicking circles on the back of her head, mixing hair and mud together like Betty Crocker's Brownie Mix when she adds water and stirs by hand 250 strokes. She counted as she rubbed, making each circle a one, beginning at the top of her head and ending there, rubbing with eyes still closed, not thinking that they couldn't see her face and it wouldn't matter if she cried.

Time has a way of bumping forward for Molly almost as giddy and quick as it slides into memory. She watches while her own hand moves the tip of a fine long-handled brush across white paper, the bristles of this brush made from ear hair of pigs. This other Molly is painting a shapely, red-mouthed woman, red hair filled with sunlight and ribbons blowing Christmas winds from hot countries, from the sea. Colors and sunlight so bright the girl in the pig pen squints behind her closed eyes. She is painting now the woman's emerald green dress that flows to the forest floor and rests in tide pools filled with lichen and soft gray and brown-celled things too small for names. Now she paints the clean, round pinkness of a young pig that nestles in pure contentment in the arms of the woman in the emerald dress, a tiny smile playing on the full red lips of the woman and a similar smile on the mouth of the pig.

Old Molly. Feeling fine resting in a hog waller.

She groped beneath her, feeling the soreness of young bruises, and grinned without opening her mouth, thinking what her friend Georgena would say. "Don't you open nothin' till I wipes your face!" Molly was of the opinion that at that moment she was sitting in the friendliest place on the farm and might as well stay there till Georgena and Lilly and Arthur got home from beauty parlor day.

She hummed that Beatles song she'd practically grown up with, the one she sang with Georgena and Lilly in the Methodist church. "Let it be / let it be / let it be / let it be ... " she trailed off.

Donald Ray James, who drove the propane truck for Southern States, had told Miss Helen when he delivered the last load, "Those peace people don't mean nothin' to me! Don't know their butt from third base, if you know what I mean." Miss Helen wouldn't let him on the place after that.

Then Sonny Boy'd gone off to Vietnam and Buffalo moved out and her periods had started. Old Pawpaw'd died on her, too, and her chest buds started growing. She had used to think Donald Ray was the finest friend a girl could have, and she believed she could actually grow up like Peter Pan, maybe even be able to finally reach her elbow with her mouth. Lilly said if she kissed her elbow she's turn into a boy for certain. As she saw it that would solve practically all of her problems.

Donald Ray looked at her funny these days, and she decided she didn't like riding the route with him high up in the truck cab with the radio on the seat between them moaning Aretha Franklin. "Chain chain chain," said the radio. Donald Ray's teeth were turning brown since he started chewing and spitting.

"Chain of fools is what I call them Yankee peace people and black butts and hippies," he told her, grinning as they bounced over a gravel farm road. She puzzled on these things when there was no one safe to talk to. Donald Ray hadn't been safe.

"Donald Ray scares me," she had told Georgena and Lilly that night, frightened and wondering at what had been so fixed in the world. Like the dirt beneath her bottom — turning to mud.

What was it about hippies and Vietnam and Black Panthers that had made Buffalo so mad he'd actually shot his 12-gauge through their new cherry TV console one night after the Huntley-Brinkley boys told the news?

"I had to get the anger out," he told her. She hadn't seen him so hot since that bastard John L. Lewis organized the coal miners.

"Piggie, Piggie, Piggie," sing-songed the boys. "Get up, Piggie!" That was Pud's baby squeal. "Getup, getup, getuuuuup. Piggie, Piggie, Piggie."

Then Lee Roy's voice, "I'm gonna go get Mama! You better get yourself out of there . . . turd face!"

The singers picked it up, giggling little boy smut, ear tops ripening like summer tomatoes, singing, "Turdface, turdface, turdface!" Not knowing for certain what a turdface was, they sang humiliation and degradation in raw tonalities, they sang boyhood in mud ball thrown. They sang pompous righteousness. Oh, piss on older brothers, with Red Ryder holsters, silver-barreled pistols lashed to thigh bone and jeans tucked into cowboy boots below.

"Damn it!" Molly said exasperatedly to the pigs. But the shoat and sow merely shuffled for a better view, neither of them smiling. Throwing back her head she roared to the sky, "I didn't do nothin'!" To the pigs she added, "I just fell, and you know that. Anybody could of."

The screen door slapped as Lee Roy went after Miss Helen. She pictured her mama sitting on the piano bench drinking bourbon and water from a short glass and staring at the red high-heel shoe which, just two days ago, for reasons not clear now, she had embedded in the picture tube.

Lee Roy hollered over his holder, "Come on, Mama! Hurry!" Miss Helen would be right behind him if she was coming, and Lee Roy would be pointing his hard knuckled finger across the lawn, through the barbed wire fence and the barn yard, to where Molly sat in the rain in the hog wallow.

"See, Mama, see?"

Her mother laughed, not unkindly, a cultured, almost amused laugh. She said something to the boys, but Molly couldn't make it out; a good sign. Miss Helen made a point of not raising her voice, but if she'd been drinking too long rules got broke. You never could tell.

Molly heard the crunch of Sonny Boy's Chevrolet Bel Aire turning into the driveway and the broom straw sound of wet tires braking on gravel. As Arthur rolled down the window, the smells of permanent wave lotion cleaned the air and Georgena's voice snapped like a mean turtle. "Go on! Get her out of there THIS MINUTE! Hook up the hose and get some of that mud off before you bring her on my porch." And just to make sure he did, she pushed Arthur off the seat into the rain. Then the car door bammed, and there was Arthur, smiling at Molly from the fence, a roll of dazzling white clothesline clutched in his fist.

That evening the kitchen radio moaned, "I'm here to get my baby out of jail." Plink Plink Plink, said the guitar. "A woman gone simpleminded over some worthless used car thief sounds like to me," says Georgena.

"Arthur! Change that radio station back where we had it," commanded Lilly.

The sky pinked over Redbud and the far-off Mississippi bottom land, and Molly gazed at the yellow bug light spilling through Lilly's kitchen window onto the soggy lawn like a broken egg. The sky was exactly the color of a pig Molly vaguely recalled.

"Been visioning again, haven't you, honey?" Georgena asked softly. Like reading her mind.

"How'd you know?" she said, giving the glider a push.

"I just know," said Georgena.

About that time the last raindrop fell and the three friends moved together in the green glider and life was lovely. Lilly made sassafras tea and served it from the fat blue and white tea pot that had a picture of a near-naked man chasing a near-naked woman around and around its bulging side. There were some pieces of old nightgown covering the nakedness but Molly could see right through it to the nipples on the woman and on the man a tiny penis that looked like your thumb does when you squeeze it between your first two fingers and pretend you've pulled it off the other thumb in a trick. Men? she thought. I don't see what Miss Helen makes such a big deal about.

Blood for Blood
Henry Riekert

The soldiers stood over the bodies and looked at them and then at each other. They were rubbing together their gloved hands and blowing on them—their breath showing like heavy smoke in the icy air—and each soldier saw himself lying among the bodies of the citizens that had been shot earlier in the day. The lieutenant had ordered the soldiers to bury the bodies though the ground was frozen hard. They had tried to tell the lieutenant, yet he could only curse and threaten to shoot them if the grave was not dug.

"It is necessary to dig only one grave," the lieutenant had told them. "One big grave to put all the bodies in, and there are only a dozen or so. It will be easy to dig or easy to die. You choose which."

But the ground was frozen and they could only scrape up a foot or less of topsoil. Now they stood looking at one another, shivering, and thinking about being shot by the lieutenant and the men he would bring back from patrol.

"He will shoot us if we do not do what he has ordered," said the first soldier. "We must bury them."

"Or bury the lieutenant," said the second soldier.

"Hush, you fool," snapped the third soldier. "You will get us shot for sure by speaking such things. We must bury the bodies if we have to use the grenades to do it."

"Gheorgie, you might have something there. Why not use the grenades to dig the graves? At least we can use them to break through the top layer of soil. It is the most frozen."

"Don't talk foolishness," said Gheorgie Druca. "I was joking about the grenades. Have we not drawn enough attention to our deeds today? And what will the lieutenant have to say about the noise we will make? No, it is foolish. We must try digging again. We must do it!"

Nicholas Lucia had been listening to the others speak. He was blowing warm breath into his gloved hands and listening. Finally, after no more was said, and they all stood and looked at each other again, he said to them, "We cannot dig and we know it. The ground is too frozen. Gheorgie, do we have the cans of petrol in the supply truck still?"

"I believe so. Why do you ask, Nicholas?"

"We must put the bodies into a pile and pour the petrol over them and burn them up. The fire will thaw the ground enough to bury what is left."

The soldiers said nothing but looked to each other for something. They were looking for someone to agree that such a horrible thing was the right thing to do. Each one was waiting for someone else to speak up and say it was right, so they could get on with it. They were all very young, none of them being older than twenty-three, except for Josef Peteskeleau; he was forty, and not like them. He was new to the unit, and the others suspected him to be a member of the secret police.

"That is stupid," said Peteskeleau. "Do you not think the fire will draw attention? Aye, you are a fool."

Peteskeleau had been the first to open fire upon the protestors earlier in the day when the orders to do so had been shouted. He did not hesitate, or give pained looks to the soldiers next to him, as the other soldiers had done, nor had he fired over the heads of the demonstrators as the other soldiers had arranged. They had worked it out before that they would not kill their countrymen if ordered to do so. They had agreed, but Peteskeleau had not. He had called the other soldiers traitors. Afterward, when they had dragged the corpses and stacked them in the back of the military truck and were riding into the country to dispose of the bodies, he had sat in the back of the truck eating his supper of Russian black bread and rat cheese and laughing at the rest of them for not having an appetite.

"Aye," said the first soldier. "If we must do it, let it be done. We have no other choice. It is a good idea for a very bad situation."

"It is stupid," said Peteskeleau.

"It is not stupid. It is you who is stupid. What do you want? For us to be shot? Will you tell the lieutenant that if not for the rest of us, you would have buried the bodies? Will you then help shoot us, Peteskeleau?"

"You are a pig!"

"No, Peteskeleau, you are the pig. Do you hear me? A fat, ugly, mean pig, and some day someone will butcher you like the pig you are!"

"I will kill you, Druca!" screamed Peteskeleau, and he pulled out a knife and lunged at him.

"Stop it, you fools," shouted Nicholas. He and the others stepped out and grabbed the two angry men and held them back from each other.

"We are going to do as I say," said Nicholas Lucia. "May God in heaven forgive us, but we have to do it. They are dead. It is nothing to do it. We let them be shot, and we watched it. For that, God will judge us. They are dead. But this is nothing."

The soldiers looked at Peteskeleau with hatred.

"And think of it, Peteskeleau," said the first soldier, who had him by the arm. "You can warm yourself while you watch your fellow citizens roast. The kind of man you are, you will somehow find it satisfying."

"Pig. I will kill you, too."

"Enough, enough," said Nicholas. "We do not have the time to fight among ourselves. We must finish this. Gheorgie, go and fetch the petrol. Do it now."

Gheorgie slowly released Peteskeleau, turned and went to the truck. The other soldiers let go of Peteskeleau and stepped back, keeping an eye on the man and not trusting him. Andre Sterlovich sat on a tree stump, rocking back and forth, staring away behind glazed-over eyes, not hearing, not seeing. He had been that way since coming from Sibiu.

Gheorgie returned carrying two twenty-liter petrol cans. Nicholas took them from Gheorgie and sat them down in front of Peteskeleau. "You do it."

Peteskeleau's eyes opened up full of anger and he screamed, "You are not my superior. I take no orders from you or anyone else here. You can go to hell."

"Yes, I can indeed. But not before you finish this."

Peteskeleau hesitated, not because he had any qualms about burning the bodies of citizens that were filled with bullets from his gun; he did not like being told to do it by Nicholas. "You can go to hell." He moved toward Nicholas menacingly. "I will teach you to try and order me around. I will teach you good."

Nicholas drew his pistol. "I will happily shoot you, comrade, if you do not do what I tell you, and if you come one step closer." He reached up and chambered a round in the CZ75. The other soldiers—except for Andre Sterlovich, who still sat rocking, unknowing—raised their rifles and leveled them on Peteskeleau. "There are two types of individuals in every revolution and in every war," said Nicholas. "He who loves freedom, and he who loves murder. We know which one you are."

Peteskeleau looked at all of them and then laughed. "Words, Lucia. Big words. Yes, you have me now. I will do as you say. You have it on me now. I will not argue." He bent down and picked up the cans and carried them over to the bodies. "I have a better idea. Let's let Andre light the fire." Peteskeleau laughed again. "He will not know what he is doing."

"Leave him alone," said Nicholas. "Andre is a good boy. He never wanted any of this. He never hurt anyone. He is more sensitive than the rest of us. He could not even stand to see what he saw today."

Peteskeleau picked up a can of petrol. "He is a woman. No stomach. He belongs in a kitchen with an apron tied to him."

"Peteskeleau," said one of the young soldiers with tears in his eyes. "You should not have poisoned the well. You shot them and that was wrong, but you should not have poisoned the well."

"Oh, go to hell," snapped Peteskeleau. "I am sick of your righteousness. You are no better than me. No better, do you hear? You say I am a murderer; I say you are a traitor."

"I would rather be a traitor than a murderer."

Peteskeleau held the young soldier in a wild, insane stare and said, "I will urinate on you when you are dead."

"Look, Nicholas, the others are returning," said Gheorgie. "We are in for it now. What are we going to do?"

Nicholas turned to see soldiers coming down the hill out of the woods. But Nicholas sensed something was not right. He did not recognize the men nor did he see the lieutenant. Nicholas turned back to his men to warn them to be on guard, but before he could speak, gunfire exploded. The men coming down the hill were charging and firing upon Nicholas and his men. Nicholas Lucia was dropped by a stream of bullets.

Gheorgie Druca was felled next after Nicholas. He had not

had time to lift his rifle in self-defense, or even to drop it and throw up his hands in surrender as the others had done. It would have done no good. Even Andre Sterlovich, who had made no other gesture save for his gentle swaying back and forth, was shot off the tree stump upon which he sat.

Peteskeleau stood frozen, with his arms reaching up for the heavens, his eyes squeezed shut, fully expecting at any moment to die. He did not want to die. He was screaming, "Please do not shoot me! Please!"

The gunfire died out and he heard footsteps all around him, men running. He opened his eyes and saw Nicholas and the others lying on the ground scattered about. The soldiers from the woods had shot every one but Peteskeleau.

Peteskeleau did not recognize these soldiers, yet they were familiar. He could not place them. He watched them move from body to body, rolling each one over, making sure every one was dead. Peteskeleau was afraid as he watched. He had been afraid to die and now he was afraid to be alive. He did not know what these men intended. If he was to be tortured to death, there was no use in rejoicing over being alive.

Then Peteskeleau recognized the men. They were citizens of Sibiu, whom he had fired upon earlier. They were relatives and friends of those whom he had killed, and whose bodies he had been about to douse with petrol. Again, thoughts of a dreadful death crept into his mind and he began to whimper. He did not want to die. He found himself trembling, and though the air was like ice, he was sweating profusely. Peteskeleau realized that he was a dead man not yet dead.

He began begging. "Please, please, please do not kill me. Please, please, please."

One of the men stepped forward. "Easy, friend," he said. "We will not hurt you. We do not hurt heroes of the revolution."

"What?" said Peteskeleau, incredulous.

"My name is Dimitri Yolania. I, along with the rest of these men, am from the village of Sibiu. Earlier today, we were attacked by government troops. We were attacked and many of our loved ones were killed simply because we marched for freedom. We were unarmed, yet we were gunned down by cowards. As if that was not enough, they poisoned the village well..."

"And my wife and baby drank from the well and died!"

said one of the men, his face twisted by rage and grief. "They poisoned innocents!"

Peteskeleau looked at the man nervously. He was fearful that this was some sort of game they were playing with him. Peteskeleau was sure that if it was a game, it would be this man's knife he would feel against his throat first.

Dimitri Yolania walked over to the pile of frozen bodies of his fellow villagers. Yolania bend down and said, "My brother, my brother. Dead."

"My brothers are there, too," said another man. "All three of them."

Peteskeleau wanted to shout for them to stop this madness. He hated the cruel things that they were doing to his mind.

Dimitri Yolania stood up and ran to Peteskeleau, who cringed and flung up his arms to shield himself. But Dimitri did not harm him. Instead, he threw his arms around Peteskeleau and hugged him. Peteskeleau was dumbfounded. He wondered if maybe he had died and this was retribution.

"You are a hero," said Dimitri Yolania. "We saw how you defied the others. We saw how they held you prisoner. We know that there were soldiers who fired over us and not at us. Do you think that we do not know the reason they held their guns on you? We understand that they had somehow found you out.

"After the attack on our village, we followed the soldiers, hoping for a chance to take blood for blood. When they split up, we ambushed a patrol and killed them and took their uniforms. Then we came for the others. That is when we came upon you and saw the murderers forcing you to pour petrol on the bodies of our loved ones. We saw how you hesitated and argued."

So that was it, though Peteskeleau. They had come upon the soldiers holding their guns on him and misunderstood. They had come up late and did not listen to, or could not hear, what was being said and did not understand.

Peteskeleau's eyes brightened and he could not contain his cackling. "Yes, yes, you are right. They made me come here after they shot your people. I shot over your heads and they discovered it. I begged of them, 'Please do not shoot them. They are our countrymen, they are of our blood.' They threatened to kill me if I did not shoot the citizens of Sibiu. But I shot no one. I fired over their heads and they discovered it. Then they tried to make me burn the bodies here to destroy their evil.

But I would not do it. I would not burn the bodies of our martyrs. I am sure they would have shot me had you not come along. Bless you, bless all of you." He stepped forward and clasped Dimitri Yolania and kissed his cheeks. "Thank you, thank you," said the blustering Peteskeleau.

"It is not necessary to thank me when it is you who is a hero. We will return to Sibiu and honor you after we have mourned our dead. You must come so that we may honor you. You must bring your family to Sibiu so that they may see you being honored."

Peteskeleau suppressed a laugh. He wanted to howl at these men, whom he considered fools. They were too stupid to know that they had just killed the very soldiers who had saved their miserable lives and thus, saved the one who had done the killing.

Peteskeleau was so happy, he wanted to dance. He knew a secret. He wanted to share it with them but it was they who held the guns and not he. He would have to find the right time to tell them. It was too good a secret to keep to himself. He was sure that they would find it amusing. He could hardly wait to tell them, to see the look upon their faces.

He would get to urinate on Nicholas and the others after all. He would cut off parts of their bodies and save them as mementos. They would be his trophies. He would kill these men, too, if it served him and the opportunity arose. He would kill them, right after he had let them in on his little secret. They deserved to die; they were nothing but idiots. Like that stupid Andre Sterlovich, who was an idiot before Sibiu and an even bigger idiot afterward. It was so funny; to them, he was their hero. He would put on a performance worthy of the theater. He would play their hero and take from it everything he could.

Peteskeleau stepped back, bowed, and said, "I will be honored to return to your village with you. But I can bring no family. I have no family. They are all dead. The good people of our country are my family. I have always tried to protect them as best I could. I am truly honored by . . ."

Peteskeleau's prattle was interrupted by the crack of a rifle, and though he showed no sign of harm—looking as if he were deep in thought, staring blankly at Dimitri Yolania but not saying anything—he slowly sank to his knees, as if preparing to receive absolution, then fell forward flat onto his face. On the ground behind Peteskeleau lay the mortally wounded Andre

Sterlovich with a just-fired rifle beside him. He looked at the lump on the ground that had been Peteskeleau, and whispered feebly, "God bless the revolution," though no one could understand what he said.

One of the citizens aimed his AK-47 at Andre and fired.

"Aye," cried the man who had shot Andre dead. "When will the good stop dying? When will the madness end?" He pointed to where Andre lay and said, "They are nothing but back-shooters." He bent down over Peteskeleau and felt for a pulse but found none. "He is dead. Another brave hero dead."

Yolania shook his head. "God forgive us. It is terrible. I do not ever want to live to see again what I have seen today. It was necessary to die and to kill others for liberty, and it is not finished yet, but I am sick of it and pray for it to end." He stared down at the body of Peteskeleau. "Put him in the truck with our people. We will take him back with us and honor him with a spot in our cemetery along side our loved ones. It is the least we can do for him."

"What about these others, Dimitri? What are we to do with them?"

Dimitri Yolania thought for a moment while looking down at Nicholas Lucia. He looked at the two cans of petrol and thought about it. Then he said, "Burn them."

Josef Peteskeleau was taken back to Sibiu and buried between Yolania's brother, whom he had shot, and the mother and child who had drunk from the poisoned well. And every Sunday for a long time afterward the townspeople prayed for them and went to put flowers on their graves.

Ghost of the Piano
Peggy Steele

There is a piano that exists only in the abstract, kind of a ghost of a piano. It can take on changeable forms. Sometimes a pianist can sit down even to the defeated old upright in a small church, a piano worn down by voices so strengthened and simplified on conviction that they have overwhelmed its temper and taught it to sing without overtones, and still find the piano's ghost. Sometimes it seems as if middle C has been used as a file to scrape off everything soft. But the ghost of the piano can infuse even such hardened brawlers as these with full-fleshed grandeur. It can slide in through an open window or through a thick wall, and the pianist will look up without surprise and welcome it as an old friend. "Why, there you are! How nice you've come."

And in these old churches, the pianist and his friend can sing until the grain in the wood of the pews flows with sap. After they have left, the church won't be so empty. The linoleum on the floor will be flooded with original color. The light streaming in through windows, whether stained or clear, will take on a golden color, and the next time the congregation comes, it will partake of that richness, not necessarily understanding, and be the better for it.

Sermons, the mature usually discover, make very little difference.

In Alaton, the piano teacher didn't have much money. The fathers and mothers paid only the spiritual teachers of their children well, the preacher who scared or reassured them according to need, the education director, whose job it was to keep the birds and bees in a jar, and a few others who tried to keep the lid on.

While they were teaching my spirit expensive lessons all day on Sunday and half the nights of the week, I was going quietly to Mrs. Wyn's house twice a week in the afternoon for that small extra, music lessons, with which my mother hoped to ice the cake.

It would be appropriate here to describe her living room for you, make all the little objects real enough to delight you with my command of my medium. Can't. Walked through her front door twice a week for over a decade and never really saw the room. I have a hazy impression of cleanness, poorness, and darkness surrounding one cone of softened yellow light streaming over the keyboard from the accordion shade of an old floor lamp.

From my front door to hers was only two blocks. I started walking it at nine when an old upright came our way from cousins moving out of town. The oldest of them, who had inherited both the family singing voice and the family temperament, had taken a bite out of the end of one of the real ivory keys and left the wondrous shape of her neat, little teeth. Oddly enough, the strength of jaw needed to bite through ivory had more to do with suddenness of temper than with badness.

My father was alcoholic, and he was gone. My mother had a hard time making ends meet. She never paid my music bill on time. I always entered Mrs. Wyn's door ashamed, in arrears. She talked to me about it sometimes, giving me another statement she had made up, telling me just how long it had been since she had seen green.

"Snookums?" She called us all that because she never could remember our names. She looked helpless eyeing me. Neither one of us was up to dealing with my mother, who had decided I was not talented in music and asked me every now and then if I didn't want to quit.

"She said she'll pay next week," I would mumble. Mother had had an attack of suddenness the last time she saw Mrs. Wyn's bill, and sucked through her teeth loud enough to be heard all over the house. That particular bill always seemed to remind her that my father didn't help.

Mrs. Wyn may have had a mother problem, too. She lived in that three-room apartment with her mother and her daughter, a little older than I. Her marriage had been brief and ended in divorce. I suspect that she married him, whoever he was, just for his name. What else can you do, if your mother's name is

Mrs. Battle?

Embarrassment over the late check is part of why I never saw her room. I was atremble with shyness, abashed. I never admitted in all that youthful decade that I wanted to use the bathroom. Only once was I ever in it. Mrs. Wyn sent me because my hands were too grubby for her keyboard.

"Let me see that face," she said, after I was settled on her bench.

I faced her, eyes down.

"Now, Snookums," she said, "I thought you promised me last time to wash your face and hands before you came. She picked up one of my limp hands and examined it. "Such pretty hands," she said. "You should take care of them."

The door by the piano which had always been closed, was opened, and I walked through a dark bedroom to a little bathroom by the back door with Mrs. Wyn, Mrs. Battle, and the daughter all standing stock still, watching me. There never was a more timid threatener to whatever tight secrecy they guarded.

Why didn't I quit lessons?

Because I had already seen the ghost of the piano. And I think Mrs. Wyn had seen it, too.

I believe the ghost of the piano is ancient; it probably was before the world was standing. When it comes into a room — and I believe it favors especially the poor rooms, the old pianos, and maybe even the poor people, the Miltons born to go unsung — it comes like a jet current in the ocean. The pianist who has been floating along on the medium of time like everybody else will find in a twinkling that he's been carried out so fast and so far to a strange new sea that both nothing and everything he ever was told before pertains. The electricity thumps so fast through his brain that some of the ordinary channels are burned out completely. The ones opened up lead to seas uncharted and unglimpsed by our self-assured, pipe-chomping, one-dimensional, scientific, wealthy, empirical psychologists. Whatever they may think, the darlings, Jacob does still occasionally let his ladder down.

When I close my eyes and remember her now, Mrs. Wyn blends into that marvelous Chinese sculpture, seven hundred years old, called "The Happy Boy," though none of her features were oriental. It's the frozen gaiety that they have in common. She was never witty. In fact, she rarely laughed. The gaiety was in the lineaments of her body and in the civilized control with which she turned her head. She was one of the only persons in town who hadn't been hit by Baptist lightning and galvanized into passionate posturings for the benefit of the Almighty and, one can't help suspecting, for the opposite sex. Living in a hotbed, she was as cool, remote, perfect, and untouchable as a Mozart melody. She seems now a very precious artifact handed down to us from a broader culture than our own. She was, of course, despised in Alaton.

On the wall above her as she taught were two black silhouettes, open work enclosed in two circles, her and her mother in profile facing each other. The very outline of Mrs. Wyn's head looked happy, balanced on the curving point of an open neckline, tilted back as in an upward gaze. The small nose, clear and upturned, seemed questioning and eager rather than snooty, and the roundedness of chin, forehead, neckline was agreeable and mild. Mrs. Battle's profile had angularity and uprightness.

"Mrs. Battle slept between them," it was often said to explain Mrs. Wyn's long-ago divorce.

"She hit my fingers with that baton whenever I played a wrong note," ex-students vowed, the many who hadn't measured up. For somehow, inexplicably, she managed to make people feel they were on trial as she stood looking up to them so carefully and mildly, making sure she understood whatever they'd said exactly. I realize now she was very shy. Then, I thought she was critical. Most of the adults I knew watched her walk off and said knowingly to one another, "Tookie." In our lingo, that meant prissy, persnickety, and small, somehow, all in one.

There was a witchy old woman piano teacher with hair dyed so unearthly black bats might have flown out of it. They loved her. She taught all her students to bang out "The Black Hawk Waltz" *fortissimo*. And they liked the little man with buckteeth whose suits were always a size too small. He'd rise on his toes with his fingers in his collar, trying to get a little extra air. His students picked up his Hungarian accent, which he had brought with him all the way from Opp, just up the road. And dear Mrs. Tittle, who could make the big organ in church sound like a calliope and bring visions of small, fat merry-go-round horses into every head, even playing staid Lutheran hymns. It was assumed that she was the town's really superior teacher, having learned her craft through sheer inspiration. She was unadulterated by anybody's instruction.

Mrs. Wyn, playing strictly by the note with too much fidelity and too little gall, never won their admiration.

I pray there is a special heaven for the millions of quiet, threadbare men of this world who have sat many midnights pushing patient red pens over student essays. Correcting spelling, grammar, logic, and rhetoric with intense, comprehensive thoughtfulness; they have managed to sweeten and order the bitter chaos of human minds just enough to keep a trace of sanity moving from generation to generation, from war to war. Beside them should sit the mild, rotund women who have pacified hundreds of their neighbors' dirty urchins, hot on their piano bench from a baseball game, into respect, and sometimes love, of music. Squirming hard in the total chaos of wanting to go, I have heard Mrs. Wyn's calm, unimpassioned voice over the rush of youth in my ears.

"Now, Snookums, you're in the key of D sharp." She'd lean forward toward the music where my eyes were locked, trying to get me to look at her. I wouldn't. Then she'd do the one thing which could always command my attention. She'd play the phrase. I would hear the notes. And I heard something else, too. If she pressed only one key with one finger, I heard it. The ghost of the piano.

It was as if standing against the wall behind her piano there was a second pair of harps like a golden shadow. When she pressed a key, the hammer fell cleanly through the ordinary world and brought a full sound from those deep strings. The gypsies speak of the gift of second sight. Perhaps the gift I speak of is a form of it. The phrase she brought forth might have been delivered out of heaven. Round. Full. Timed so accurately between velvety black silences that it existed like a softened spotlight on a darkened stage. That bristle of sharps became a reality, and worlds behind that one may have celebrated the redemption of one small sinner. I was enchanted.

But still, I couldn't look at her — that glassy wall of constraint — though she still fished to catch my eyes. It was embarrassing to hear a phrase so rich. Anyhow, I still didn't know the names of all those sharps and that, after all, is what we both thought she wanted to teach me. I think, even now, that if my eyes had begun to shine a reflection of the radiance I felt, she would have become embarrassed, too. We were focused on the paper, the keyboard, the hands. We were right there in her ordinary, one-dimensional living room, not prepared to be swept out to sea.

I might come back the next week able to play the phrase gracefully with a touch now and then on those deep strings. I would know only from her stillness that she heard it, too. Once, I played "Near You" on those deep strings, and she said, with a bewildered look on her face, "Snookums, you almost make me like that piece." That was as close as she ever came to telling me what lay beyond the notes we both looked at as we talked to one another, but it was close enough, I guess, to keep me believing.

Neither one of us, however, could stay in her calm living room. Both of us frequently had to go to church. I was in training as a Christian soldier. She was church organist and pianist, trying to earn her bread.

She couldn't play to suit the choir director. At choir practice, it was as if time stopped flowing gently, minute by minute past. Time became solid, chopped up in sections like stage sets. Ezra would stretch his eyes as wide as they would go, open his immense mouth, swoop his hands up high, and the choir would suck up half the air in the room and hold it with unbelievable bosoms. He'd wriggle his Ichabod fingers at Mrs. Wyn, and she'd give us an introduction with no ballyhoo. She played the notes quietly, exactly as they were written in the hymnal, precision-timed, jarring us with their correctness. He'd drop his hands, deflating the choir, and tell her with exaggerated politeness to go a little faster. He would snap his fingers to demonstrate. A whole lot faster.

She could precision-time the sixteenth notes no matter how fast he set the pace, and she could get all the notes written, too, no matter how awful the key or how clumsy the chords. Her fair skin would go bright red, whether from exertion or disagreement or shyness, nobody ever knew.

Ezra would pump his elbows, pulling her and the choir along, turning all the sixteenth notes into triplets, all the mouths into megaphones, and all the individuals into a mob. Except for one. She just turned more scarlet and more blue-eyed, and more tightly score-bound in an agony of musicianly integrity.

In that sea of allegory my youth has come to be, Mrs. Wyn bobbles up, mostly, I think, to be forgiven her terrifying correctness.

I traveled back that way once on a Greyhound bus, a long

ride that took all night. I got to Alaton at seven in the morning and stepped out to a shining new bus station built on her old street. I placed myself instantly, though all the houses on her block were gone. I imagined her house, one side covered by an old kudzu vine.

Her exact house site was easy to trace. It lay at the edge of the Greyhound paving. Parts of the stucco-like foundation remained, concrete larded with pebbles, and the kudzu vine had survived, lightly, to cover the entire lot, delicate, nebulous leaves on a vine imported, the scientists claim by terrible error in judgment, from Japan. There, it is an annual, planted every spring to give a buoyant nitrogen to the depleted old soil. Hard Japanese winters kill its roots each year. But in Alaton the almost coastal soil is rich. The winter is easy, and rules concerning temperatures and likelihoods don't altogether hold true. The kudzu disappears each December without a trace, but like all things so delicate that bulldozers don't apply, it finds a way each spring to lift its flat leaves, not very high off the ground. Rippling like water in the sunlight, it keeps green the piano's ghost, lying under that ground like springwater waiting to be tapped.

Walls tumble down somewhere and the years begin to merge. These lovely things that happened so long ago are still lovely and potent, brimming up from the allegorical waters like bright fish rich with life. They free my hands to stretch out more fully to the people in my world today. My mind rests like a becalmed ship on whatever waters these are, grateful for the other fishers, enchanted with all the traffic by the sea. The tyranny of time is banished. Beethoven is as vibrant on my record player as he was writing scores in Bonn. All the dancers who ever danced on all the stages are still dancing.

Barking Dogs
David Stewart

The mountain was the only place he felt comfortable. It stifled him to travel between rolling hills or through dark, tall forests. Even staring out across rice paddies didn't give him the sense of the horizon. Something was always in the way, blocking his view. He missed the endless stretch of Kansas sky.

Approaching the mountain was like approaching a great, lost cathedral rising out of the Asian jungle. It was strewn with climbing vines and soaring flights of granite that guided men's eyes toward the holy heights. The peak was a place of majesty and peace, a refuge from the daily life below. He could see green vistas from his throne on top of the mountain. The green changed gradually to grey and then to blue as the hills rolled to the horizon in all directions.

His throne was solid, living rock. Tons of hard, grey stone carved at the beginnings of the world by an ancient deity. A back and arms formed around him, rounded and smoothed by the ages. The stone's mass radiated against his hot skin, cooling him with the breath of the mountain core, making him a part of the earth. And he could see forever.

It was a perfect night. Comfortable. Bugs cleared by the breeze. Lights of the town at the foot of the mountain, each as bright and vivid as the glint of a sharp blade. The glimmer of full, round moonlight on the river winding through the distance. Clouds drifting in the lunar stillness cast shadows like trees in a summer field. He heard a dog barking at a ghost creeping near a farm house. No, that was just his imagination. There were other sounds, but no dogs. A French balloonist had written in the early days of manned flight that a dog's bark was the last sound heard at great heights. Prisoners in dank cells clawed at the sills of tiny, barred windows to pull themselves up and hear the dogs in the night. The tiny people in this warring land ate dogs. A vision of the fleshy grin of a skinned carcass lying on a bloodied bed of its own hide filled his mind. Spread like a lover offering all in blind trust. The thought repulsed him.

Zeus's throne swung gently under Artemis' great white globe. The wind blew warmly about him, driving him along with the cloud shadows, the landscape passing beneath his feet. People below lived their lives, vaguely aware of his presence. Loving. Birthing. Dying. Killing. When he wanted, he would seep into men's subconscious, honed from ancient, primeval beginnings to be aware of God's presence. Not to understand it. Just to sense it. Enough to stir and shift in the presence of the heavenly attention, lured in their prayers or their sleep to the Olympian threshold.

He felt a sudden presence and heard a foot on the rock. There was no threat. Even with a war going on, he was comfortable in his place at the crown of the mountain, ringed by the Aresian community of warriors.

"Out praying, Preacher Man?"

"Just watching the world go by. You?" He had to crane his neck to look behind him at the voice.

"It's a beautiful night, isn't it? So quiet and peaceful."

Johnson moved and stood next to him so they shared the vision of the shadowed vista.

"What's the matter," he asked Zeus. "Can't you sleep?"

"No, I didn't want to miss the quiet. Things get so busy in the daytime. No time to think. What are you doing up?"

"Thought I'd work the perimeter a little before I go to bed. Play at war. Spook the gooks, if any are up to mischief. You want to call the shots?"

"No. I'll just watch. You want to borrow my radio?"

Johnson laughed. "Never thought I'd see an artillery man give up the throttle. Sure. It'll save me going after mine."

Zeus picked up the radio with a metallic scrape from its place next to the throne and swung it onto his lap. In the darkness he found the switch and twisted it. The handset was cool against his ear.

"Mighty Stallion Zero Niner. Mighty Stallion Zero Niner. This is Mighty Stallion One Four. Radio check, please."

A small, still voice spoke in his ear.

"It works," he told Johnson. "Have fun."

Johnson picked his way among the scattered rocks in the white moonlight. The rocks were easy to see. It was the shadow of a rock that presented a potential hazard. His blond hair stood out against his bronzed skin like the crest of a helmet. The two men had the same blond bulk though Zeus was taller. They were the largest men on the mountain. They shared the blueness of eye, too. Eyes so blue they spoke of power, conviction, and confidence. So piercing they could make the guilty cower. So piercing they commanded more attention than any rank given by men.

Johnson chose a spot on the Green Line a stone's throw from the throne, between a bunker and the latrine. The Green Line circled the area below Zeus's throne, outlined by oil drums filled with rock and studded with sand-bagged bunkers. Inside the circle were other bunkers, bristling with men who fed on war. Johnson's choice was a point where the mountain was easier to scale. The area posed a threat to the men nestled in the barbed wire nest, like birds of prey awaiting the dawn to hunt again.

Zeus stretched forth his hand and blessed Johnson's efforts. He was a warrior thrusting his spear into the bushes around the camp to flush out the enemy before they could harm the men under his command, his care. A father protecting his sons.

Johnson gave back to his men what he demanded of them, Zeus thought. Loyalty, strength, single-mindedness. The skilled practice of war. He offered them his life, taking the same risks, sharing the same hardships. Johnson was looked up to like a god by his men. No, not a full god. He was a man, rooted in the earth, born of woman, but conceived by a god. Men would not function with a real god in their midst. They needed someone mortal to guide their lives. Someone with the same flesh and blood but with a divine core. Achilles had been like that. Men feared gods but respected other men with the ability to rise above shared weakness and pain to take charge of their lives. That ability, Zeus knew, was the only true link between heaven and earth.

Now all he could see of Johnson was his shadow. A spirit, he thought. A wraith from hell, dealing death with fire and brimstone. The crossing at the bar delivered to the souls looking for a way into the perimeter. Repent, O Sinners, he willed.

The first round was a surprise, hitting with a metallic crash in the trees below. The hillside dropped too quickly for the Son of Cronos to see the round strike, but Johnson's shadow lightened in his vision and sank back into darkness like a match struck and blown out.

Another shadow walked out of a bunker, passing close to Johnson. The shadow paused, merging with Johnson's shadow. The shadows split apart like a cell dividing. One moved to the latrine. The tin-covered door slammed, leaving Johnson alone.

The next round dropped into place. Then the next. Johnson is good, Zeus thought. The rounds worked back and forth like a stream of fire splattering on parched earth. Thunderbolts from heaven.

This is a rude surprise, Zeus thought, for anyone crawling around in the trees below. The Son of Cronos reached into Johnson's mind, discovered the logic, and waited for the next barrage to drop farther down the mountain, chasing the little men bolting through the jungle.

Johnson started. Zeus felt it. His mind recognized the change in pattern before it understood what was causing the change. At the speed of light, he dove to the foot of the throne, prostrating himself like a sinner begging forgiveness.

The artillery round hit the dirt at the side of the bunker. Shrapnel hissed and whined past him, horrible with its potential for random violence. The sound of dirt and stones whispering down around him followed before he could take a breath. He heard Johnson yelling like he didn't need a radio to contact the distant guns.

"Cease firing! Cease firing!"

The Son of Cronos jumped over the rocks to the Green Line, pulling a flashlight from his pocket as he flew. The latrine door banged open and a form fell out onto the packed dirt, tripping over the pants gathered about its ankles. Zeus shone his light on the form, its chest opened by the shrapnel. Gaping eyes, glistening blood, gasping for breath. Save me, Father, the boy mouthed to him.

Johnson rushed to his knees beside the form. "God! I've killed him! O God in Heaven, I've killed my own man!"

The boy's feet kicked and he reached for Johnson like he was reaching for life or holding off death. His belt buckle flapped and rattled around his ankles. Zeus was surprised in the sudden quiet that followed a moment later. Feet running toward them reminded him of falling debris.

"O God, what am I going to do?" It was a prayer without a deity.

Johnson looked up at the Son of Cronos. Zeus knew the boy was gone from the way Johnson sat back.

"Can you say a prayer, Preacher Man?" Johnson asked in a way that said he wanted a miracle.

Zeus pushed the horror out of his mind. He gathered his wits and searched for the soul hovering over them. He heard the hounds rushing through the gates of hell in full cry like a flash flood tumbling and flowing with black fur. They snapped and snarled at each other with slavering jaws in the fight to be at the head of the pack. The smell of the wavering soul filled the glistening, cavernous nostrils.

"Into Your hands, O merciful Savior, we commend Your servant. Acknowledge, we humbly beseech You, a sheep of Your own fold, a lamb of Your own flock, a sinner of Your own redeeming. Receive him into the arms of Your mercy, into the blessed rest of everlasting peace, and into the glorious company of the saints in light. Amen."

The Son of Cronos heard the dogs driven back from their bone, fearful and disappointed but still fighting among themselves. He felt the brilliance of the heavenly host about him. The boy's soul, harvested by salvation, pulled gently away to the rising chorus. The night gathered back around him, hissing and rolling like a wave of ebony rushing onto the shore. He became aware of the crowd of panting men staring at Johnson crying over the boy.

Zeus sat on his throne in the bright morning sunlight. The sun had first risen over a field of clouds that stretched to the horizon, as firm, as smooth, as dense as new fallen snow on a plain. As the sun warmed, the mist dissipated, melting into the surrounding air, exposing the lush green life in the world below. Tiny cars traveled up and down the main street of the town. An automatic weapon rattled, quick and muted by distance, so suddenly that Zeus couldn't trace its source in the field of melting snow. He wondered if small arms fire could be heard from a higher altitude than a barking dog.

He had watched the activity from his throne throughout the night as the boy's body was examined, wrapped in rubber, and carried to the idling chopper. Only a stain in the scuffed dirt remained outside the latrine door. Footprints already passed through the stain.

One of the investigating officers had talked with him to get the details. After that, Zeus descended and found Johnson sitting in his bunker. He prayed with Johnson, watched his quiet, anguished ravings.

That man will go mad, the Son of Cronos thought later as the activity around his throne died down. He will be destroyed.

Then it was peaceful and quiet again. He went into a reverie that carried him with the smiling moon until dawn. The horror of death was replaced by the satisfaction of having kept his head. He had quoted a passage from the *Book of Common Prayer* by memory. He hadn't thought of it in over a year. God had planted it in his mind, to sprout in the need of the moment, to grow as a balm in the breasts of those who heard it.

This was why he had left the seminary. He felt the call. God didn't want him to wait to be formally ordained. He obeyed. His friends were stunned that he would express his conviction by joining the army they were protesting against. They abandoned him one by one, until only Carole was left. Carole of the fair face and fiery ways, Carole who loved him, who stood up to riot police with him, who cried in the rolling clouds of tear gas with him. After their first march together, she had told him, her eyebrow arched, that the "e" added to her name stood for "erotic."

"Someone has to be there to save the souls," he explained to her stricken silence. It was their last meal together. "I must help heal the wounds of the heart. My protest against the war won't end it. People will still die. And they'll still need salvation. God has called me to leave you to dispense his grace. My call isn't to stay and protest the war."

He watched the pain in her face change to anger, the brimming tears replaced by flashes of light. He had seen the flashes of light in their marches over the year.

"How can you fight evil by becoming part of it?" she hissed in his face.

Zeus felt doubt creep in around the edges of his resolve like mold on bread crust, tainting the soft, pure white of his righteousness. He had anticipated sorrow. Certainly he had understood her tears. But he hadn't expected anger, especially not Carole's. She surely knew how deeply his convictions ran, how well thought out they were.

"The war is evil, brought about by men who have lost their way." In his mind, his own way seemed indistinct, his argument muddled, blunted by her vehemence. He pushed on as though his litany, rehearsed over and over in his mind and in his prayers at the chapel altar, would clarify his path. "But it's fought by others who are the prisoners of the system. They see themselves as having no choice but to fight. Or else they see the war like it was a big football game. They imagine coming home a hero and claiming the cheerleader."

Carole looked hard at him. She wasn't afraid to look into his blue eyes.

"You're missing the point," she snapped. "If we stop the war, these boys won't have to go. They can stay home and play their football games."

"No, you're the one missing the point." Zeus felt his frustration rising. Praying in the chapel, this had all seemed so clear. What was the matter with this woman?

"The war won't stop tomorrow," he pressed. "My face will be missing from the protest, but the Establishment won't notice. In just a little while, I'll be helping real people in Vietnam, not fighting a faceless bureaucracy in Washington. Your voice will still rise in the streets. Together, you and I can make a difference."

"No, not together. I'm going to have to face this one alone. You're lost and you don't even know it."

Carole sat for a moment longer. Her eyes were brown, not blue. Then she left, pulling the noise and clatter of the busy restaurant out the door into the street with her. Leaving him with only silent, questioning glances.

Zeus sat stone-faced and prayed for guidance. How could a relationship so intimate, so nurtured since the first day after class, so intensely centered on the good of mankind disappear into a busy street in the breath of a moment? Surely this must have been the pain Christ felt as he prayed in the garden near his sleeping disciples. Zeus was the one making the sacrifice, risking his life, leaving the comforts of home behind.

As the sounds of the crowd around him picked back up, he felt the flood of heavenly peace again. At that moment, he was reaffirmed. He needed to be on the front lines, day in and day out, if he was to serve those who needed him most. Chaplains in the rear were like pastors who never left the pulpit.

The radio on the arm of his throne spoke to him like a small spirit bearing a message. He picked up the mike.
"This is Mighty Stallion One Four. Go ahead, please."
"One Four, I have a report of enemy movement. Looking at my map, you should be able to give me a visual from your position. I have firm coordinates. Are you ready to copy?"
Zeus pulled a notebook from his pocket and fished a pencil out of the spiralled wire. "Mighty Stallion Zero Niner. This is One Four. I'm prepared to copy."
He copied the strings of numbers. Keys to human lives. At the intersection of these tiny digits, fate hung on a cross.
A chance to save a life by taking a life. At first the dichotomy had bothered him. Kill them, save us. He wanted to help relieve the suffering, not cause it. But God had sent him to the thickest part of the suffering where he was needed. Where he was needed to serve God's will. As a healer. And as an avenger. As whatever God saw fit. He was a tool. An extension of God's own arm. He could serve only by being a participant, not a bystander.
At the side of the throne was his map. Stiff with cardboard and plastic. A window on the world. He loved maps for that very reason.
As a child he had enjoyed the maps in the *National Geographic* magazines more than the pictures of people or animals. He would set up a trip across Africa or Asia or the Middle East. Then he imagined his daily progress from start to finish. Colored flags with numbers marked the extent of each day's journey. The difficulties and their resolutions were all worked out in his head. He imagined the weeping concern of his parents as he struck out on each journey and the cheering, admiring crowds as he reached his goal. He read about Speake, Hillary, and Halliburton. He imagined taking his place with the heroes. He had imagined young boys bursting with satisfaction as they read about his own journeys and conquests.
In the army, maps took on a third dimension, depth. The fine black lines that snaked around the contours of the earth gave a reality to his wandering eyes. The maps became a true picture of his world, deep enough to lose himself. Hills, valleys, plains, plateaus all became intimately immediate. Real. An extended vision of what he could see from his throne.

Reaching from the sea to Cambodia.

He followed the numbered grids across the map until he had isolated a box. Then he imagined the box being divided into tenths. He isolated a section of the river beyond the town. He divided the box in his mind again, counting with the point of his pencil. As he stopped, the point pressed into the map at a spot on the river. Two hills sat on either side, gently swelling like the young breasts of a naiad with a blue necklace nestled between them.

"One Four, this is Zero Niner. Have you located the target?"

"This is One Four. Affirmative. Let me see if I can get a visual. Stand by."

Zeus's spotting scope stood over him on a tripod like a long-legged bird, searching the horizon.

The vision of the breasts leaped through the glass-filled passages of the tubes leading to his eyes. He adjusted the focus and concentrated on the river. A tiny dot appeared like a gnat on a surface that was brown and speckled with light. He blinked and studied the tiny boat, a vee spreading from its stern. The men in it were almost too tiny to matter. The sampan, with whatever illicit cargo it carried, would be the target of opportunity.

"Niner. This is One Four. Visual confirmed. Fire mission."

The Son of Cronos intoned the incantation that brought the thunderbolts, the proof of his wrath.

"Round out." Niner's voice used the same inflection as if repeating a prayer memorized in childhood.

The plume of water was behind the craft. Zeus spoke the incantation again.

"Round out," Niner prayed responsively.

The spray of water was close enough to capsize the boat.

"Fire for effect," Zeus intoned. Feel the wrath of God, he thought.

Five more bolts struck the river. Poseidon, God of the Sea, Earthshaker, Brother of Zeus, stuck his fork in the boiling muck and stirred, leaving it churning like a boiling stew.

"Cease firing," commanded the Minister of Destiny, his voice booming with righteousness.

Tiny bits of flotsam bobbed in the calming river. Parts of the sampan. Or perhaps the men, he thought. Suddenly he heard the dogs rushing out of the gates of hell again. Let them come, he thought.

"Mission accomplished, Niner."

"That's a roger, One Four. We're going to send out a bird with a team to see what they can find. I'll call you back with the results."

Zeus imagined the dead men dragged out onto the slimy river bank, slick with mud. Sprawling in the mud with their arms thrown wide, legs spread.

"Roger, Niner. One Four out."

How interesting, the Son of Cronos thought, to witness these deaths separated by just twelve hours. One by accident, the others by design, all by the same bolt of lightning. He had dispensed mercy and justice with equal ability. All it took was the proper set of instructions. He settled back into his throne. Allowing himself to be an extension of God's will was just a matter of being willing to submit his own will to God.

"Mighty Stallion One Four, this is Mighty Stallion Zero Niner. Come in, please."

"Go ahead, Niner."

"The team confirmed three KIA. It turns out it was three kids, the town mayor's son and two friends out for a little fishing. They wandered into a free fire zone by mistake. The CO and the chaplain are headed for town to pay their respects."

"Roger, Zero Niner. Appreciate the news. Tough luck." Zeus felt chilled. Numb. As though the stone he sat in had pulled the warmth of life from him.

"By the way, One Four. The old man said you'd still get credited for three kills. It's an ill wind that blows no man good, right?"

The other gods hung around the throne and shouted at each other. Eris, also called Strife, the sister of Ares, had some sort of disagreement with Persephone. Everyone else took sides and threw in their arguments. It was getting on his nerves. Suddenly Iris, the Rainbow, announced it was time to eat. The group bustled down the hall away from the throne. Persephone and Eris were still going at it.

The Son of Cronos was relieved by the quiet. The polished marble floor reflected him looking at himself. His glance followed a trail of sunlight across the floor to a window, bright and cold beyond the latticework. The branches of a naked tree scratched against the glass like a dead man desperate to leave hell.

Squeaking shoes marched up the polished aisle toward him. Zeus jerked his head away, pretending he didn't see the orderly coming toward him. All he wanted was to be left in the quiet.

"Hey! Preacher Man! How come you're not in the cafeteria? Come on, man. You can't sit here and starve to death. Where'd you get that damn wheelchair, Preacher Man? Thou shalt not steal, right? Shit, man, you trying to act like you're wounded or something?"

Zeus stared straight ahead.

"Come on, Preacher Man. You're not too big for me to help. Give me your hand. I'll pull you up and we'll walk together."

Zeus stared straight ahead.

"Oh, what the hell. Sit tight and I'll roll you to the cafeteria. You won't have to raise a finger or lift a foot. Like a regular king. Like a regular, goddamned king."

The orderly disappeared behind Zeus and he felt the man's breath ruffle his hair. The floor began to slip away beneath his feet. He remembered what the French balloonist had said about the bark of a dog. What a pleasure it would be to hear a dog bark again. Just once more.

One Main Sound
Mary Ann Taylor-Hall

The truck skidded. I ran, getting nowhere, still hanging onto some foolish piece of laundry, a flowered pillowcase. The truck skidded silently into the dogwood tree. My body opened to a big empty scream, *Molly*. The scream turned to glass, nothing in it, no child.

I went back to work, a week or so later, after everybody had come and gone. I didn't plan it. I just found myself in front of the bathroom mirror, the first night I was alone again in the house, pulling my hair all to one side, shoving in the combs. My fingers were ice cold. I put my fiddle in its case, got in the car, and drove to Justice's.

"Well," Cap said into the mike. He ducked his head, strummed his guitar a little bit, checking it sideways with TJ's bass. Then he turned back and leaned the mike toward his mouth a little. "We got Karin back." He let go of the mike and looked over at me without smiling and let everyone clap and whistle. We have our regulars there now. I guess they knew the story. I tucked my fiddle under my chin. He nodded, and, my heart thudding, I arched my shoulders up and brought us into the rousing melody of "Brown County Breakdown."

The fingers of my left hand flew through the patterns; they didn't have to think. My bow waited, then plunged forward over the strings, ducking and dancing, bright sixteenths to take your mind off how music rushes ahead, weaving and rollicking, through the tics and tocs of the time there is in this world. I waited, all wired up, for my turn to leap in there. I sent my bow singing up the strings, over the melody, reaching high and beautiful, or I was down underneath it, in the serious ranges. I worked little soft *arpeggios* in around the words Cap and Joyner and Louis sang.

There were nights during this time when I had the feeling *I* was the bow. My whole body sliding sideways, just this side of a faint.

They were right behind me. They watched out for me, they were careful what they played, no "Six More Miles to the Graveyard." Not that it mattered — I couldn't hold words in my mind. "I want to play, but I'm not singing, Cap," I told him, that first night back. He nodded. "Fine. That's fine."

Cap, he's as ancient as this place he comes from. His face is from early times, the flat thrifty way it's made, with nothing extra, the spare lips, the sharp nose that has the slight break to it just below the bridge, like the line of one of these ridges out here, the brow not high but from temple-to-temple broad, the bleached eyebrows, the long lines down the cheeks that come from a hard life, too much weather. All his muscles are economical and well-developed, even in his lower arms and hands, from his strong playing on that old Dreadnaught. Veins run through his fingers and up his arms. I'll tell you, there have been times when I have just wanted to lick the path they took. I didn't want anyone but him, he wanted everybody but me, a situation that gave me a lot of nervous energy for a while.

There have been times when love sat in my throat, right where you swallow. I couldn't eat. But I could still sing. We sang hot songs, might as well put all that misery to good use. He lifted my voice, brought it out, loved around it on the refrains. It was as though he wanted to be invisible then, to everybody but me. Our two voices slid together trustfully, they were of one mind. His voice found the right place for itself against mine, locked onto mine like radar, through every last little edgy turn. It was like dancing. Or worse. You can go a long way just on harmony.

His body is an authority on many subjects. It knows exactly what to do with itself — except when it comes to me, his old buddy Karin. I stopped paying attention to it a long time ago. I stamped my desire down into friendliness. With my cute cowboy boots. I had other opportunities. I took advantage of one of them. That's where Molly came from. I chose her father for his genes — he was some kind of kin to old Fiddlin' John Carson. Just passing through.

When I went back to work, after the accident, I forgot about

Cap. I couldn't keep my mind on him. He was the lead guitar, period. All I could keep my mind on was the music.

One main sound, somebody said, that first night. We were sitting at a long table between sets, drinking beer. If somebody said something funny, everybody's eyes would slide sideways to see if I was laughing. I laughed, Lord. I couldn't talk, but my smile felt hooked to my ears. A woman I hadn't seen before sat with her arm around Louis's shoulders. She blew out smoke and said, "If you concentrate you can kind of hear it." I strained to catch what she was saying. "And pretty soon, you hear it all the time, underneath everything." We all got real quiet, trying to hear it under George Jones on the jukeox. "One main sound, so they say."

That night I went home and sat against the wall. I tried to hear it. I heard a high tingling buzz. I wondered if that's what she meant.

One main sound. It made sense, it figured. There's one main light in the world; everything we call color is a splitting apart of this one light. So I thought maybe there might be one great chord, too, like the light of the sun, that separates into the notes of the world. Creation would be the splitting apart of this chord. Music would come out of it, every note, every harmony. Music would also try to get back to it.

It was just an idea, but the idea excited me. I seemed to know what it meant; it drew me, it comforted me.

I didn't hear it, not that night. The next night I did — just for a moment, but I was sure of what I heard. A way-off steady chord, a full, low G major, I'd say. Resonant and harmonic.

Then that was what I did. It was my work. Listening. I latched onto the idea of it.

I would come home from Justice's, or wherever, at night. I would undress in the dark and put on my bathrobe and sit against the cool plaster, listening, till the light came. Then I'd get myself something to eat, unplug the phone and go to bed. I'd sleep, on and off — it was never a really deep sleep, but I figured it was easier on me to come awake not screaming in the daylight than in the dark. I'd get up in the afternoon and practice for a couple of hours, then somebody would show up — they had it divvied out by days of the week, I guess — to fix dinner and eat with me. Then I'd get myself dressed and go play at Justice's. We'd play our three sets, then I'd come home.

And sit against the wall again, trying to hear the one sound. That was the work I was doing then.

It went on for several weeks. The sound did finally seem to encompass everything. The names did finally fall away from things. I don't know, I guess I was hallucinating by then. When I looked at the thing we call *table*, I couldn't remember the name of it, didn't even want to. What was important was the sound it gave off, a solid, steady particular sound in the one ongoing chord.

I'm just trying to reach back and say what it was like. I can't make it happen now, though it happens every once in a while in spite of me.

Everything was within it, myself and my dead child and every breath every breather ever breathed.

I guess I needed to hear it.

Cars would go by in the street, a siren far off. The fraternity on the corner had parties with loud music; wind blew through the maple tree, carrying the heavy back beat with it. A branch would brush the roof, or somebody on the street would call out. These separate incidental sounds of the world going on seemed like rocks that the river of the one main sound flowed around. Or like flashes of light thrown off of it. I began to think of it as a river. I was on its banks.

On its banks. The ground under my feet was this: There was no way in the world out of what had happened; it was final. I would never see her again.

I would hear it. Then I would go play my fiddle with Cap and Joyner and Louis and TJ. One night, right in the middle of "Sallie Gooden," I heard the sound. Playing was like bidding the notes to rise up out of it, one at a time, flash and shake themselves, then go back.

So I heard the music a new way. This hearing gave my playing a definiteness, a clean certainty, a brilliance it hadn't had before. I had to concentrate; I had to keep the one sound in mind the whole time I was calling the separate notes out of it.

I was further from singing than I'd ever been.

I kept my mouth shut and played to save my soul. They gave me room, they cleared out a place in the music for me and let me have my head. They didn't look at me after I finished a riff. I'd sort of drift back and disappear. Joyner would step up quick to his mike through the applause and quiet it with that banjo-picking of his that sounds like wild horses, to take everybody's minds off what they'd just heard. Or old poker-face Louis would crawl inside that dobro and break it loose. Then we'd all be in it again, and Cap and Joyner and Louis would sing one last chorus. Then we'd all step back and finally take quick sidelong glances at each other, fall to tuning or adjusting capos or taking care of busted strings, getting ready for the next number, Cap chatting the audience up while we did it, joking with Joyner like nothing unusual at all was happening. "Might ought to tune this thing," he'd say, and Joyner would come back, "Why mess with it now? We was all just about to get adjusted."

I smiled and joked around, I smiled and drank my beer, and all the time, I swear, that sound was looming underneath everything. Vast, harmonic, taking in everything. I smiled, sliding sideways, the big glissando, like a leaf sliding on the wind, down and down and down, while Cap and Joyner put their heads together and sang, *Some sweet day they'll turn me loose, from this dirty old callaboose.*

And then I'd go home to listen again.

If I could have sat there a little longer. If Cap hadn't come after me that night.

Sometimes I lost it, of course. I had to sit perfectly still for a long time sometimes. So when I got it, I would try to hold onto it. It held onto *me*. It folded around me, it gave me peace. It didn't matter so much then, this business of being alive or being dead. When I could keep hearing it for a long enough time, it would lift me up out of my grief-struck body. I would feel myself not just connected to but somehow part of the same thing Molly was part of. And I would be light.

But Cap came and rescued me.

I don't try to hear it anymore. I understand the danger, for me. But sometimes when I'm tired, it will come over me, the way an uncatchable rush of a dream from the night before will come over me when I turn down the covers to get back into bed.

I sat against the wall. Then I slept or tried to. Then I practiced, first the precise lonely singing of the scales, then the figures. I would break them apart, studying the bowing. Some of these old jig figures, slow them down and they'll break your heart. I would fill the little house with sounds of my own making.

Then I would go meet the band. We were all playing

beyond our abilities. It was a miracle, and we all knew it, though nobody mentioned it, except to say, once in a while, "Damn, that sounded good to me."

Then I'd go home and lean against the wall. That listening was the hardest work I'd ever done. Tougher than learning the fiddle, even. Nothing dreamy or absentminded about it.

The darkness was full of high hums, buzzes, cracks, flutters, roars. Then these fell away, or blended. Or were overcome. Toward the end, my own breathing was incidental, detached from me, far off.

A deep rushing, I wanted it. The image of lowering myself into it came to me. I began to think I had a choice in the matter. Thinking I had a choice helped me, made it possible for me to sleep. I'd sleep then, a dreamless dark sleep, as far as I knew, no grief no death no loss. And when I woke, there would be at first some momentous relief, elation, as though Molly and I were together. No separation, she was with me.

The grief would come upon me later, as I picked up my fiddle, as I drew the bow over the strings. That low grieving sound of the violin. That high wild singing, and it would gather again. But I would discipline it to the scales, to the figure of the jig and hornpipe, to a grave, full tone.

So I gave my life over to music, and to the sound music came out of.

A roar, a low powerful continuous rushing noise—a river, unstoppable steady swift.

There came a time about a month after I went back to play with the band when I didn't want to practice when I woke. I pressed my face into her clothes, still hanging in the closet.

I slid down the wall next to her closet, to try to hear the sound. It was a thirst, an addiction. Need entered in. I needed to enter that current.

When somebody showed up at my front door, with flowers, food, tapes, I would put water on for tea. I would listen hard to words. I would nod, smile, say some words myself. I wasn't able to let the words into my understanding. "*Talk* to me, Karin," my friend Martha would say. "I'm all right," I'd say. "Like hell you are." "No, really. Don't baby me."

I thought I was all right. I'd get myself over to Justice's on the nights we played there. Afterwards, I drove home fast, as soon as I could leave, with the radio turned off. I knew what I wanted.

Better to want the melodies. The clever progressions, temporal arrangements. Since we have to live in time. Can't live outside of it. I know that now.

The deep swift current. It was just a matter of getting up the courage. A grave ongoing sound by then, a roar. It would get quieter when it went through the rocks to where Molly was. It would be as quiet then again as the heart of music.

If I could get out into the middle of it, I understood it would take me to my girl. It would carry me beyond the pale. Beyond the curb, into the street, where I had found her, and beyond that place, then, too.

The one most dark full sound. If I could be inside it, not just listening to it —

The sound of blood, coursing through the universe. All I needed to do was to leave the bank. On the surface it could be still, but swift underneath. The other river, underneath.

I got dressed in my jeans and red silk blouse, my brown boots. I put on my earrings. I tried to put on my stage makeup, looking at my faraway face in the mirror. I didn't stop, exactly. I just couldn't make myself hurry up, even though it was getting late.

I'll just sit down for a minute, I'll jut sit down on the floor for a minute. I'll just lean back against the wall for a minute, and listen. It didn't matter if I was late, none of that mattered. *I'll just close my eyes for a minute.*

I got out into the middle of it. It was easy. I just stepped out. I let it take me. I didn't breathe, the sound breathed around me, it was partly made of breath.

I don't know what happened. Time passed, I guess.

Some rocks came that the sound had to separate and flow around. Six. They rocked my body. Then when I thought I was past that place, six more. And I thought, this is the rocky place I have to go through to get to her.

Loud sounds I thought I should see about. But they didn't matter. Loud definite sounds from the place I couldn't remember, like: no! no! no! no!

Then hard sounds coming through the rooms of the house. I saw the sharp U-shape of each one come down. Cap leaned toward me with a look on his face as though he'd found me lying in a pool of blood.

My red silk blouse.

Pool of silence.

If I'd known what was happening sooner, I could have gotten out the back door, run for my life.

He knelt on the floor beside me. He said my name. I remembered it was mine. *Karin.*

What would have happened if he hadn't come? Would I have died there? Of what ? Would I have literally opened a vein? Or just flipped out, temporarily or permanently? Maybe I would have just sat there on the floor for a little longer, then gotten up and lived my life in a normal, regular, quiet way.

He knelt there, talking to me, sounding the way you do when you try to sweet-talk a cat out from under a bed.

He put his hand on my bare arm, flat at first, and then he grasped it around with his fingers. I drew back, I jerked my arm back. "Leave me *alone*," I said, but he held on. He wanted me to get up. He didn't know what he was doing. He was where he had no business to be. I heard his calm voice: "Come on, honey, you need to get up from there. " He didn't have a clue what I needed. I shut my eyes tight. I didn't want him in my sight. I felt in my fingers how I would choke him for interrupting me, for saying my name. I was way past the field of gravity of his take-charge voice and sexy eyes and black cowboy jacket. "I want you to leave me alone, Cap," I said. "I want you to back off." My voice felt chiseled.

His fear was in his hand tighter than he would have wanted. "All right, Karin," he said. "But I'm staying. If you need me I'm right here." I didn't need him. He went somewhere a little way off, taking the bad-memory smell of bar smoke and beer with him. I suppose he went to sleep. I thought of saying his name, but that idea left me; I forgot about him. I was far gone again into my studies. I heard him breathing, then that sound was gone, too. I was so close, so close —

But then it was first light and he was sitting on the edge of my bed putting his boots back on. I saw him, far back, a distant memory. I could hardly place him. "How long has it been since you ate?" he asked.

I knew then that my only hope was to get up off the floor and act natural, so he would leave. I found my legs, I stood up shakily. I took a shower and got dressed. He was in the kitchen, fresh as a daisy, when I came out. His jeans still had a crease in them. I wanted to ask, "Does your grandma iron them for you or do you send them to the laundry?" He put a plate of eggs in front of me; I ate them to get rid of them. I said, "I'm fine now.

Thank you. You go on now, Cap."

"I'll drop by around two-thirty. See if you can sleep some now."

"I will. You don't need to be worrying about me. You got enough to do."

He put his hands on my shoulders. His eyes moved over my face, like he was checking to see if I had a rash. "I'll be by this afternoon."

I went to the window and saw him swing up into his van and back it down the driveway. Two-thirty, then. I didn't think I'd need that long. When he was out of sight, I went right back to the bedroom, sat down where I'd been, dropped right back into it. No problem, no problem anymore.

A loud, serious working sound, like machinery now. I was getting somewhere fast. Then, to my joy and amazement, I began to think I could hear something else, behind the clanking roar — a perfect sweet silence. I can't describe the quality of it. It was like — a wide expanse of still, pure water. I think now you must hear this sound right before you die. Or right afterwards. I tell you, I could see the rocks I had to go through to get to her. I could see through them, a little, to some *beyond*. A radiance. A sweet loving shine. I was on my way, I really think I was.

As close as I'll ever get and live to tell the tale.

I don't know what was in store for me. I don't know what would have happened, what I would have done. I'm only remembering as well as I can the feeling of what I was moving toward. Freedom, peace. Still, silver water, golden light. Gathering momentum — too late to stop myself; I was into the rapids already. I surged forward, excited. I forgot everything, except that there was plenty of time, that I would know what to do, that there would be time to do it. That the way to do it would be clear to me.

Then there was Cap again, as if he came down out of thin air. I didn't know he was there until he knelt swiftly to lift me. *Too soon!* was all I could think, bitterly. A trick. (I don't know whether it was a trick or not. I'd lost track of time. It could have been 2:30, or 10:15. To this day, I can't be sure whether he lied to me. I thought at the time he had, to trick me, and I hated him for it. I really don't know. The events of that day, till evening, are a blur to me.)

He didn't talk this time, he just knelt fast to lift me. But I was fast, too. All instinct, fighting for my life. I grabbed his arms, we grappled together. I slapped him, scratched at him. I had come so far, it had been so hard, I'd had so much to learn. I was almost there, dear God! And here comes Cap, taking it upon himself to pull me back, out of the solemn, sacred current of that river. "Who the hell do you think you are?" I screamed at him.

He held me off. He warded off my slaps and kicks and struggled this way and that, till holding me off turned into holding.

Until this dead-serious wrestling turned into what I'd always wanted from him, but not then. And then I wanted it then.

I tried to stay in the current, even as I fought with him, even as he lifted me away from it. Tears running down his face. They stopped me. Tears.

I let go of it. Of the chance to go through to my girl. I let go. Like a hand unclutching, like fingers forced open.

He held me then, cradled me, rocked me. My muscles were all so tight. They'd been clenched ever since she died. His hands moved then, knowing how to help me. To help my poor old body. He put me on the bed to help me. Everything happened then, I wanted it to. The old thing with Cap, flashing out, leaping out of the darkness I had made. Grief and lust ringing against each other, like I'd swallowed a set of church bells.

Going down, sliding down. Our bodies giving in to it, at last. Easy, the pure release of it, like I'd been holding my breath for years, and then I breathed. Necessary. No keeping from it. I turned away. I turned away from that radiance and entered something else, a darkness, like the dark at the center of a plant. It closed around the two of us, the living ones.

I couldn't help it, I sank down into the mattress. The same one Molly and I had slept on together when she crawled in at night to press against me. I couldn't help it. I was pulling him down then, into that darkness that doesn't know anything but wanting and not having and having.

His grave face yielding, those lines around his mouth. His neat hard brown hands, bringing me, bringing me.

Back to life.

Come back, come back, each side called out. Each side said the other side was death. Love was on both sides. I had to choose. I chose to go back to the side I knew about.

Oh, little screamer, cheeks all flushed out. Bright Eyes, coming back for more, shrieking and swinging that feather pillow around your head, blonde tangled hair flying.

I feel I've failed her twice. I didn't look, the one time when I should have been looking. I took my eyes off of her and down the driveway she went, her legs held out from the pedals, coasting, free. And afterwards, when I almost had her in my sight, when I felt her right there waiting for me, I chose to turn back.

Those tears running down his face. Crying for everything, I guess. I held onto him for poor dear life.

Toward evening, he took me to stay with his grandma in the country. He drove with one hand, his eyes wide open in the wind, looking straight ahead. All I heard were the tires on the road, something singing in the fields, crickets. I guess. I closed my eyes and nearly slept. It was her smallness I remembered then; death made her so little. And right on top of that, a kind of dream, merciful. I dreamt I was dressing her. Combing her hair, putting on her best pink dress. It felt ceremonious, as though I were getting her ready to be married, or to take communion or something. Something religious. She stood still while I clasped her locket. She buckled her white sandals by herself over her pink socks with lace at the cuffs. She was excited. So was I. I opened my eyes then and saw all there was to see. Mackerel clouds, converging to a point in the east. White cows with the last long light of the clear day making them glow against the fields as though lit from underneath. The beginning pink of the sunset, over on the other side.

Reflections on an Abandoned House Jesse James Once Supposedly Slept In
Allison Thorpe

It's just a dumpy, old log cabin grown shaggy with years. Two brick fireplaces — tottering bookends — sandwich the tiny rooms. Chinking has crumbled and lies now like stale breadcrumbs even the blue jays won't touch. The boards are rough, thick poplar, weathered to a wrinkled blush. Broken windows, long and narrow, grin with jagged teeth. A patched roof of forgotten tin slants low over the porch eyeing westward, away from the highway. Gnarled grapevines, green rattlers, smother the north wall. Poison ivy has claimed the south. The east bows like a naked prisoner to the whip of ridge winds.

But for spring.

Come season, the old place dons a lilac gown of southern hospitality. Leafy petticoats sashay, cause the howling drafts to stutter, fall down, roll over. Year after year as I travel that same stretch of winding road on my way to a job of which I have long tired, that purple temptress sways in wait, ready to siren adventure loose from my middle-aged soul. With heady allure, the flowery perfume invades my window easily, whispering, "Slow down, come back, d-r-i-n-k m-e i-n. The stories I have to tell," it flirts as I race by. "Sit. Listen. I'll tell."

No time. I press the pedal, late as usual. The low hills teem with trucks and tractors. Ranch houses sporting pink lawn flamingos fly by. Newly graded roads, varicose veins, blur. My mind is flung to a time before the oozing asphalt, the machine violations, the three-bedroom bricks . . .

. . . the only sound: a fierce pounding of hooves as he gallops the dense valley. His breath comes harsh and ragged. Sweat pours salty raw down his face and back. Good thing this pony's stout, he thinks. Too hot a day for April. Smells ripe of August.

He curses. The shootout went all wrong. Lost his horse. Hell, what was that shaky old man doing with a gun anyway? Darn fool couldn't see a blazing thing. Hit the horse instead of him. Lucky the pony was near. They been traveling strong for a telling day now, and she ain't let up once. It's like she's been waiting for this all her weary life, and she don't aim to stop 'til she gets her fill. The dust is about to bury them though, he thinks. It's done ready to swallow them whole.

Driest spring in a hundred years, some say, and they pass more than one field resting brown and thirsty, bearing crops of honeysuckle and bent cedar. Locusts rule the world. Creeks lie dead as the animals that go there to die, dry as the windy grit between his teeth, dry as farmer bones rattling to the moneylenders waiting to bleed 'em like stones, like the stony fields. Dry as one more day to face.

The pony tosses her saucy black nose to water. He lets her lead. They wander the twists of a muddy branch to a clear, deep pool. She drinks long before the man gets down in it. Whiskey couldn't do better, he thinks, though he'd be willing to give it a try. The pony nudges him in her greed for motion.

There's something about this money they carry the pony don't like. The man knows it ain't much. He wonders what happened to the boys. He didn't see one go down—none but his horse. He curses again. This part of Kentucky was supposed to be full of small, sleepy banks. Just right for him and his men. He takes a deep breath. He needs to head for Missoura. Needs to head home.

Night comes faster than their travelings, but the moon bides them through shadow. He sees a faint glow off to the right and rubs his eyes. It doesn't go away. There shouldn't be anything out here; still, the man slows to quiet. The pony has manners enough to follow.

It's a small place out in the middle of the dark. He ties the horse to a shagbark and steals closer. The air is heavy with lilac, powerful enough to addle a man's senses. He feels lost in its savored force.

"Up easy now." The metal is ice on his neck, the voice low.

Female. "What are you up to sneaking around a person's window in the middle of the night?"

"My horse and I been riding hard," he answers. "We need a place to sleep."

"You smell like you been riding hard. I want you to turn real slow."

He moves. She is shy of five feet with hair the look and color of steel, modeling a set of red johnnys, and aiming a sawed-off barrel at his heart. Something wasn't right. Something about her eyes.

"You're blind," he says, lowering his arms.

"Keep 'em up there, sonny. Just 'cause a person's eyeballs give out don't mean they can't see! Now, who are you? Where you headed?"

What to say?

"I'm waiting."

Then, "You wouldn't be the first man I killed."

"Bob Walker. Heading out for the cattle drives."

"Ain't been cattle drives through here since . . ."

"Going to visit my brother."

"Wouldn't be traveling so fast."

"I robbed a bank."

"Now we're getting somewhere. Put your hands down and go rescue that poor horse. The barn's yonder."

He rubs and blankets the pony. Tosses hay from a tidy stack. A pair of large bays watch with curious care. An old black buggy sits tucked back in the shadows. Everything is well kept. Too well, he thinks. Must be some old man about. Sons. A blind woman couldn't do all this. He returns with a cautious step.

"I'm alone," she calls impatiently from inside, tracking his silence, reading his thoughts. "Come in, come in, there's hot food."

There is indeed. Fresh bread. Stew full of carrots, potatoes, green beans, and beef chunks big as the state of Missoura. The man laughs. He sees berry pie and cups of dark, steaming coffee. He almost forgets the old woman in his hunger.

"I like a man with an appetite. My late husband and all my boys was fine eaters. What joy to set a table full. There's tobacco in the far drawer." She shuffles toward the pantry. Brings out a bottle and pours two shots. "To them that lives outside."

"Outside what, ma'am?" he asks.

She taps his glass. Throws it back like a cowhand. "One's enough for me, but pour what you will. There's a mess of rooms down the hall."

"Front of the fire is fine with me ma'am." He draws another shot, trying to cool his parched throat. What luck, he thinks, in finding this place.

"It feels safe having a man in the house again. Can't be too careful. Not with people like Jesse James running in and out of Kentucky."

"Jesse James, huh?" He misses the glass. "I was just fooling about robbing banks." Spills on his leg.

"Well, I can see when a man's tired."

He turns away. "I'll tend to the coals."

For all his troubles, a dead sleep finds the man. When he wakes, it's with a start in the unfamiliar dimness.

"Old woman, what're you doing rustling in the night?" He smells side pork frying.

"Son, for me it's always night."

They down their fill, the woman chattering on like a morning bird. Like easy family. She hears the horse first and motions the man to stillness, but he readies his gun as she strides into the yard.

"Morning, Clem."

"Cora." The man on the big chestnut nods. "You all right this morning?" The voice is rough.

"I'm fine! And know you well enough to know you ain't come to pass the day. What's on your mind?"

"It's the James gang. They hit nearby. Heard tell Jesse headed this way."

"Clem, I keep my gun loaded and I can use it!"

"I know it, Cora. Now don't get yourself excited. I just think it's right foolish for a woman to be living out here by herself. One of these . . ."

"We been through all that," she cuts in. "I'm staying! It's mine, Clem, and I ain't leaving. Not Jesse James, not twister, not flood gonna do it!"

"He's a killer."

"I'll remember that."

The man inside hears the dust of fast hooves. Then her strong mutterings, ". . . meddlesome old goathead."

"Your beau?" he laughs.

"Oh, you shush! I got no need of a beau. I married my

mister out of love and walked his side for thirty years and six sons and outlived 'em all." She stands board straight and still against a doorway lit of red dawn. "Now I just spend every one of the Lord's days in hard work, waiting to join my family." She nods to the large stretch of lilacs out back and looks young as a dreaming girl.

The man wonders at the purple and green wildness amid the drought.

"Some days I get to wishing a body would break in and bash my head," she continues. "Shoot out my heart. Send me to the lilacs." Sighing, "I get impatient."

"I gotta go," he says.

Those sightless eyeballs stare down his soul.

"I'd give it all to buy your way in," he says a bit too loud.

They glare and glare.

"I know you would, boy. I know you would."

He shunts the moneybags atop the hay and walks out of that small haven, mounts his pony, and rides across the dry fields, up into the hills of tomorrow, and he can't get the smell of lilac from his head . . .

. . . as I drive by. Plows run rampant. Pickups whizz by my old jeep. Bulldozers raze the land.

Don't lose the lilacs, I cry.

Please, the lilacs.

About the Authors

Constance Alexander is a published poet; playwrite; award-winning newspaper columnist; and regular commentator on WKMS-FM, the National Public Radio affiliate in Murray, Kentucky. Her poetry has been published in various feminist journals and anthologies, as well as *Kentucky Poetry Review, Without Halos, Snake Nation Review,* and *The Literature of Work.* She has received playwriting grants from the Kentucky Arts Council and the Kentucky Foundation for Women; and her plays have been performed throughout Kentucky.

Garry Barker was born in 1943, grew up in Elliott and Fleming Counties, and graduated from Berea College in 1965. His books are *Fire On The Mountain,* 1983; *Copperhead Summer,* 1985; *Mountain Passage & Other Stories,* 1986; and *All Night Dog,* 1988; all from Kentucke Imprints. His 1991 history, *The Handcraft Revival In Southern Appalachia, 1930-1990,* was published by The University of Tennessee Press. He also writes "Head of the Holler," a humor column, for several Kentucky newspapers.

Chris Beyers, a poet and critic, has a study on the political dimensions of Wallace Stevens' aesthetics forthcoming in the *Wallace Stevens Journal.* He is working on an interpretation of the grammatical structure of Auden's *Spain,* and a monograph on the poetics of Barnabe Googe. He is also married to a Lexington artist who once lived across the street from James Lane Allen's childhood home.

Marjorie M. Bixler, of Jeffersontown, is a former teacher and artist. She has published stories in *The Pikeville Review* and in *Down the River: A Collection of Ohio Valley Fiction and Poetry.* She is presently working on two novels.

Pat Carr has a BA and MA from Rice, a PhD from Tulane. She's published nine books, including *The Women in the Mirror,* which won the Iowa Fiction Award, and her stories have appeared in such places as *The Southern Review, Yale Review,* and *Best American Short Stories.* In addition to the Iowa Award, she has also received a Library of Congress Marc IV, a South and West Fiction Award, an NEH, and the Texas Institute of Letters Short Story Award. She currently teaches creative writing and literature at Western Kentucky University.

Chris Holbrook is from Soft Shell, Kentucky. He received an MFA from the Iowa Writer's Workshop in 1986, and a fellowship to the Fine Arts Work Center in Provincetown, Massachusetts in 1987. He has received an Al Smith Fellowship in fiction from the Kentucky Arts Council. His stories have appeared in *Mountainside, Pavement, Shankpainter, Pine Mountain Sand and Gravel,* and *Wind.* He currently teaches at Alice Lloyd College.

Martin Kent is the pseudonym used by Mark Brewer in honor of his grandmother, who encouraged him to become a writer. He has lived in Kentucky all his life and believes that, like the character Mike, "You don't have to be black or Hispanic or homeless to be disenfranchised in America; just fail to be desirable.

Michelle Moore, of Louisville, is the recipient of a 1991 grant from the Kentucky Foundation for Women. She holds an MFA from Vermont College.

Barbara Presnell is a native North Carolinian but has lived in Kentucky for seven years. She works as an artist-in-residence for the Kentucky Arts Council, and teaches writing and literature at the University of Kentucky. She holds an MFA from UNC-Greensboro, and writes poems and plays as well as short stories.

Deborah Reed is a Lexington native. She attended the University of Florida, the New School for Social Research where she studied with Stanley Kunitz, the University of Kentucky from which she was expelled twice, and graduated from Transylvania University. She has worked editorially with Ziff-Davis Publications in New York, as a librarian in the world's largest library on beer, as an off-Broadway stage electrician, a car hop in the Deep South, and is a founder of the Lexington Farmers' Market.

Henry Riekert was born and raised in eastern Kentucky. He graduated from the University of Kentucky in 1978 and has lived in Lexington ever since. He began writing five years ago, and has had several of his short stories and essays published.

Peggy Steele is an editor of *Plainsong*. Her editorial views were profiled in the 1988 *Poet's Market*. Her work has appeared in *The American Voice, The Small Farm, Poetry Now,* and *Adena,* among other journals, and also in anthologies such as *No Known Pattern* and the *National Poetry Contest Anthology for 1988*. She has been a Fellow at the Virginia Center for the Creative Arts and the Wolf Pen Women Writers Colony. She teaches literature and creative writing courses at Western Kentucky University, and lives in Bowling Green.

David Stewart was born in Kentucky in 1947, but most of his young life was spent in the mountains of central Africa. He returned to Kentucky for high school and college. After being drafted and serving in Vietnam, he worked in Central America, and then went back to the University of Louisville to earn a degree in economics. He is working on a novel, the first chapter of which has been published by *The Louisville Review*. "Barking Dogs" is his first published short story.

Mary Ann Taylor-Hall is a writer living in Harrison County, Kentucky.

Allison Thorpe is the author of a book of poems, *Thoughts While Swinging a Wild Child in a Green Mesh Hammock."* She is the recipient of The Ladies Club Fiction Award, the Harriette Arnow Award for Fiction, and a creative writing scholarship, and is an organic gardener. Her poetry chapbook, *Swooning and Other Art Forms*, won the Edna Meudt Memorial Scholarship award. She has a story forthcoming in *Short Fiction by Women*.

Acknowledgements

We are grateful to the Kentucky Arts Council for their financial support, which helped make this book possible.

The editors of The Lexington Press (Scot Brannon, Marguerite Floyd, and Charlie Hughes) wish to extend special thanks to the manuscript readers of *Groundwater*: Sandra Baksys, Nancy Coman Covenety, Christopher Thomas King, and Matthew Vaughn. We couldn't have done it without you!

Thanks also to Sharon Lewis, Irwin Pickett, Chris King, Lynagh's, Mike Tevis, Mark Dryden, Robert Lange, Jeannie Leavell, and all the readers who volunteered their time for our fundraiser.

"Hellcat," by Garry Barker, originally appeared, in slightly different form, in *Appalachian Heritage* (May/June, 1985) and *Mountain Passage & Other Stories* (Kentucke Imprints, 1986). Reprinted by permission of the author.

"The Terrorist, " by Pat Carr, is scheduled for inclusion in a book of her short stories forthcoming from Nightshade Press.

"Making It Through the Night," by Barbara Presnell, was originally published in *Iowa Woman*, volume 9, number 4.

The excerpt from Deborah Reed's "Scenic Roots" first appeared in *Heartworks: A Celebration of Kentucky Writing*, 1992. Reprinted by permission of the author.

"One Main Sound," by Mary Ann Taylor-Hall, originally appeared in *Ploughshares*, Winter 1990-91. Reprinted by permission of the author.

"Reflections on the House Jesse James Once Supposedly Slept In," by Allison Thorpe, first appeared in *Zephyrus*, Spring 1990. Reprinted by permission of the author.